"I've been nothing [...] you."

Brenna dragged in a breath, scented with Josh's citrusy aftershave, and shook her head. "You're no trouble..."

His arms tightened around her, pulling her closer. His heart pounded fast and hard; she could feel the beat of it in sync with hers. "You don't sound convinced." He eased away slightly. "You worked so hard on the wedding and reception."

"Maybe it's not turning out so badly," she said. Then her breath caught as she realized her faux pas. "I mean—for everyone else. Obviously it hasn't for you."

"Brenna..." He slid his fingertips along her cheekbone to the curve of her jaw. Her skin tingled everywhere he'd touched her.

His blue eyes darkening, he murmured, "Maybe it's not turning out so badly for me either." Then he leaned forward, as if he intended to kiss her.

Dear Reader,

I hope you've been enjoying my American Romance miniseries, THE WEDDING PARTY. But if *Forever His Bride* is the first book you're reading, don't worry. You'll have no problem following along as all four books happen simultaneously. I'm having so much fun writing this series.

The heroine of *Forever His Bride*, Brenna Kelly, is very special to me because I've been her—the bridesmaid with the biggest dress size. (Note to self: never agree to be bridesmaid for a Barbie-size bride with all Barbie-size friends. Except me.) Brenna is self-confident, strong and perfectly content with her body. She wouldn't crash diet or try to jog herself into a smaller dress. (I shouldn't have either; my knee still hurts.) I found so much satisfaction writing *Forever His Bride* where the *real* woman gets the perfect guy. Brenna is my heroine. I hope she'll be yours, too.

Happy Reading!

Lisa Childs

Forever His Bride

LISA CHILDS

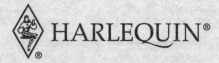

HARLEQUIN®

TORONTO • NEW YORK • LONDON
AMSTERDAM • PARIS • SYDNEY • HAMBURG
STOCKHOLM • ATHENS • TOKYO • MILAN • MADRID
PRAGUE • WARSAW • BUDAPEST • AUCKLAND

ISBN-13: 978-0-373-75226-3
ISBN-10:   0-373-75226-1

FOREVER HIS BRIDE

www.eHarlequin.com

Printed in U.S.A.

ABOUT THE AUTHOR

Bestselling, award-winning author Lisa Childs writes paranormal and contemporary romance for Harlequin/Silhouette Books. She lives on thirty acres in west Michigan with her husband, two daughters, a talkative Siamese and a long-haired Chihuahua who thinks she's a rottweiler. Lisa loves hearing from readers, who can contact her through her Web site, www.lisachilds.com, or snail mail address, P.O. Box 139, Marne, MI 49435.

Books by Lisa Childs

HARLEQUIN AMERICAN ROMANCE
1198—UNEXPECTED BRIDE*
1210—THE BEST MAN'S BRIDE*

HARLEQUIN INTRIGUE
664—RETURN OF THE LAWMAN
720—SARAH'S SECRETS
758—BRIDAL RECONNAISSANCE
834—THE SUBSTITUTE SISTER

HARLEQUIN NEXT
TAKING BACK MARY ELLEN BLACK
LEARNING TO HULA
CHRISTMAS PRESENCE
  "Secret Santa"

*The Wedding Party

To Al & Kim—couldn't have gotten this one done
without your help! Thank you!!!

Chapter One

As the first notes of the wedding march played, Dr. Joshua Towers closed his eyes. His gut twisted, and a wave of dizziness washed over him. God, he'd made a mistake. *A terrible mistake.*

The music stuttered, the verse died away, and a murmur arose from the guests. Had the old lady playing the organ had a heart attack? He lifted his lids and looked over at the woman, who wore a wide-brimmed hat bedecked with flowers. Although her hands were frozen above the keys of the old organ, she appeared fine. Her gaze met his, then slid away.

Josh turned toward the pews in front of him, noting all the people watching him as he waited at the altar. Like the organist, their gazes dropped from his. *What the hell...?* Weren't they supposed to be facing the back of the church, where the bride was about to come down the aisle, holding the arm of her older brother, who was giving her away?

But Molly's brother stood alone in the aisle. Unlike everyone else, Clayton McClintock wasn't staring at Josh. The dark-haired man focused instead on one of the bridesmaids, probably the blonde. Josh turned toward the bridesmaids, too, but his attention was drawn to the red-haired maid of honor.

Brenna Kelly returned his look, her wide green eyes warm with concern. For him? Despite weeks of e-mails and phone calls regarding the wedding, she barely knew Josh. But then again, she probably knew him better than his bride did. Brenna had been the one handling the wedding details. He'd thought his bride had been too busy, but maybe she just hadn't cared. Did Brenna Kelly care?

As she drew in a shaky breath, her breasts strained the bodice of her strapless red satin dress. The red should have clashed with her bright auburn hair, waves of which flowed around her bare shoulders. But instead the crimson satin highlighted her alabaster skin, glowing with myriad colors from the sunlight streaming through the arched stained-glass window behind them.

Guilt tightened the knots in his stomach and he closed his eyes in shame, breaking the connection between himself and Brenna Kelly. There he was, in church, about to marry another woman. It didn't matter that Molly McClintock had apparently changed her mind. Josh had no business ogling his fiancée's best friend, her maid of honor. Maybe *he* had no honor.

A hand closed around Josh's shoulder, squeezing. "God, man, I'm sorry," the best man murmured in a hoarse whisper.

Josh turned his head toward his friend and narrowed his eyes, trying to gauge Dr. Nick Jameson's sincerity. He'd known Nick since they were in preschool, and together they'd fought playground bullies, chased girls and crammed all night for tests. Because they'd known each other so long, they were more like brothers than friends, so they were always honest with each other. Nick had thought that

Josh was even crazier for proposing to a woman he hadn't known that long than he'd been in marrying his first wife, who'd left Josh when their twin boys were just babies. Nick had been right about both women. But he was such a good friend that he genuinely was sorry.

Clayton, the brother of the bride, finally tore his attention from the blond bridesmaid, Abby Hamilton. At the rehearsal dinner the Kellys had hosted, Josh had met everyone in the wedding party except for the one groomsman who'd backed out. Now Clayton addressed the guests. "The wedding is going to be slightly delayed," he announced. "The bride is not quite ready yet, so we appreciate your patience. Thank you."

Finally, his eyes full of regret, Clayton faced Josh. He knew this was not going to be just a slight delay. The bride wasn't *ever* going to be ready to marry him.

Abby, probably anxious to see if her friend was all right, took off down the aisle at a run. As Clayton caught up with her and slowed her to a trot, the music resumed. Josh's four-year-old twins, Buzz and TJ, in their black tuxedoes, ran after Abby, probably thinking a game of tag had begun. When the rest of the wedding party filed out, leaving Josh standing alone at the altar, he realized he was *it*. The loser who still couldn't catch a bride after the first one he'd caught ran away. He'd been dumped once after the altar, and now, this time, before.

A woman's hand wound through his arm, tugging him toward the aisle. He hadn't been left alone. The maid of honor led him out of the sanctuary, past all the gawking guests. While the pews on both the bride's and groom's sides were equally full, only a few of the guests were there because of him. So he wasn't too embarrassed at being stood up. In fact, his heart lifted. The pressure on his chest, which had been there ever since he'd proposed to a woman he hadn't known that well, finally eased.

BRENNA HURRIED DOWN THE AISLE, clutching the jilted groom's arm close to her side as if she could absorb the pain her friend Molly had just inflicted on him. At the same time she curved her lips into a smile, just to reassure the guests. *Everything will be all right.* She couldn't say those words to Dr. Joshua Towers, though. She couldn't say *anything* as they walked into the bride's dressing room and joined the rest of the wedding party.

Except for the bride. Molly was gone. Brenna had known that the moment Clayton appeared without her. Unlike Abby, who'd taken off down the aisle hoping to find their friend, Brenna had known right away that Molly wouldn't be nervously pacing the dressing room. When she'd shooed out her bridesmaids minutes before the ceremony was to start, Molly had been absolutely calm. Brenna had been the one riding a roller coaster of nerves and emotions—almost as if *she* were the bride. But Brenna was always the bridesmaid, never the bride.

From a hook on the dressing room wall hung Molly's wedding dress, its layers of lace and satin lifting in the warm summer breeze blowing through an open window. *Oh, Molly, what have you done?*

Molly had always been the smartest member of the group of friends, to which she, Brenna and Abby Hamilton had belonged since kindergarten. In second grade, when he'd moved to Cloverville, Michigan, Eric South had joined them. Molly had always been the most sensible of the friends: she wasn't the type to go out a window on her wedding day. She wasn't the type to accept the proposal of a man she'd only been seriously dating for a few months, either. And yet she had.

Molly's younger sister, Colleen, the tagalong of the bunch, had always been the impulsive McClintock—back when they were kids. After Mr. McClintock had died eight years ago, Colleen had restrained her impulsive nature. Hanging on to the arm of the handsome best man, however, she appeared a bit wild-eyed—as if she were wrestling some strong impulses now. And Dr. Jameson, his jaw clenched and his green eyes hard with anger, was obviously wrestling with his temper.

He wasn't the only angry one. Clayton McClintock argued with Abby. Despite the fact that she'd been gone for eight years, the minute the single mother had set foot back in Cloverville, she and Clayton had picked up where they'd left off, with their animosity barely masking the attraction for each other that they kept fighting. Brenna shook her head, wondering if they'd ever call a truce.

Abby uncrumpled a sheet of paper, apparently a note Molly had left, declaring, "It's a good thing that she ran off before making the biggest mistake of her life."

Next to her, Josh gasped. Still Brenna could say nothing; she couldn't argue with Abby's statement, not when she wholeheartedly agreed. If Molly had had any doubts, she'd had no business accepting Josh's proposal, no business setting a wedding date—and no business breaking the heart of a good man. While Brenna had never been left at the altar, she'd been stood up enough times to be able to commiserate with some of Josh's humiliation and disappointment. But she knew nothing about heartbreak. She'd never been in love.

"Josh, I'm sorry," Clayton said.

He wasn't the only one. But Brenna couldn't say the words—they stuck in her throat. She, who'd been bossing around everyone since they were kids, couldn't speak.

Abby's four-year-old daughter, Lara, dressed like a miniature bride in a lacy white dress, reprimanded her mother. "Mommy, you're not s'posed to run in church or talk loud."

"I'm sorry," Abby said, both to Josh and her daughter. "She doesn't say that in the note…about making a mistake. She's just really confused right now."

"What's going on?" asked Molly's younger brother, Rory. The teenager tugged loose the knot of his bow tie. "Did she really skip out?"

"Ask Abby," his older brother said. "She's the one with the explanation."

Abby. Not Brenna, whom Molly had asked to be her maid of honor. Guilt had tears stinging Brenna's eyes. Had Molly noticed that her maid of honor had developed feelings she had no business feeling for the groom? Even before she'd met him in person at the rehearsal dinner the night before, she'd been drawn, through phone calls and e-mail, to his wit and self-deprecating humor.

And his kindness.

"Is she all right?" Josh asked about his runaway bride. His deep voice held only concern, not a trace of anger.

"She's okay," Abby assured him. "She's just confused right now. She needs some time alone to figure out what she really wants."

Brenna thought she understood why, for the first time in her life, Molly McClintock had acted on impulse, temporarily put on hold her plan of becoming a doctor and accepted Dr. Joshua Towers's proposal of marriage.

His hair was nearly as black as his tux except for the glints of blue that shimmered under the fluorescent lights. His eyes echoed the deep blue. With his tall, muscular build and finely chiseled face, Dr. Towers was easily the handsomest man Brenna had ever met. Not that there were all that many handsome, eligible men in this small town where Brenna had grown up and to which she had returned, after college, to manage the family bakery.

But Josh wasn't eligible, Brenna reminded herself. Even though his bride might have taken off, they were still engaged, still involved. He loved her. He must love her, or why had he proposed?

WHILE THE OTHERS TALKED, Josh focused his attention on his sons, kicking himself for having set them up for more disappointment. First their mother had deserted them, and now their almost-stepmother. A smile tugged at his lips as he watched the two. They actually didn't seem that upset. Buzz and TJ plucked petals off each other's boutonnieres. Bits of red carnations dropped like confetti onto the beige carpeting.

She loves me. She loves me not. Definitely not.

But, hell, he hadn't loved her either—not in the way a man should love the woman he was marrying. He had proposed because he'd thought he *could* love her like that, since he already cared for her as a friend. Molly was beautiful and smart, with a generous nature, and he'd enjoyed the time he'd spent with her—when their crazy schedules had allowed.

He'd thought that a relationship built on friendship first would be stronger and last longer than one built on lust. Like his first marriage—although he'd been so infatuated with Amy that he'd thought it was love at the time. And that had ended with his becoming a single father.

After that fiasco, he should have known better than to rush into another relationship. Molly had been smart to leave him at the altar. He didn't deserve the sympathetic looks the rest of the wedding party kept casting his way, especially the maid of honor. Her green eyes warm with sympathy, she seemed more upset for him than his best man did. But Nick was just pissed—probably as much *at* Josh as *for* him.

Josh had convinced Nick to open the private practice, which they'd talked about since they were premed, here in Cloverville. It hadn't been easy to sell his friend, who'd only ever lived in cities, on starting a business in the small town of Cloverville. But because of their friendship, Nick finally had agreed, albeit begrudgingly.

"Maybe she should have figured *that* out before she accepted Josh's proposal," Nick griped, referring to Molly's need to decide what she wanted. "It's pretty damned flaky to back out at the altar."

"Molly is not flaky," the bride's younger sister, Colleen, defended her.

Josh had to agree. "It's my fault," he admitted. "I rushed her into this, even though I knew she wasn't ready."

Nick squeezed his shoulder reassuringly. "Don't blame yourself. She could have told you no. This just goes to show you, they can't be trusted."

Once Nick calmed down, he would undoubtedly rub in that "I told you so." Josh deserved it, too. It wasn't the women who couldn't be trusted, though—it was Josh's judgment. He'd developed the unfortunate habit of picking the wrong ones. Or maybe he'd just never come across the right one. Until now?

He glanced sideways at Brenna Kelly, who'd been quiet since the bride had failed to walk down the aisle. She'd worked so hard on the wedding—far harder than Josh, who'd been busy with the boys and work, and harder than the bride, who'd been busy finishing up school—or putting it on hold and closing up her campus apartment. He wasn't exactly sure what his bride had been doing. But he knew what Brenna had been doing—working her ass off to make this day special for her best friend. She had to be upset. Guilt, over being relieved that the bride had bailed, twisted his gut.

When Mrs. McClintock and the others began to squabble over whether or not they should cancel the reception, Josh agreed with the woman who'd almost been his mother-in-law. Her reasons for not canceling were that everything was paid for, so many people had worked hard on the preparations and she didn't want to disappoint the townspeople who'd been anticipating a party.

Josh's reason was Brenna. He didn't want to disappoint *her.*

JOSH SQUINTED AGAINST the sunlight as he followed the boys outside the church, leaving everyone else inside. Clayton had taken it upon himself to make the announcement to the guests that the wedding was off, but Josh still had to make the announcement to his sons.

"Race you down the stairs," TJ challenged his brother.

"Wait, boys," he said as he settled on the top step of the stairs leading down to the sidewalk. "Sit with me a minute."

The twins exchanged one of their glances, speaking to each other without words, and joined him. Perhaps they hadn't been as oblivious to what had gone on in the church as he'd thought.

"Are you okay, Daddy?" Buzz asked, putting his hand on Josh's shoulder much as Nick, his namesake, had in the church. Buzz had earned his nickname only a couple of years ago, after he'd gotten hold of Josh's razor. His hair had been kept "buzzed" short ever since he'd given himself that first haircut. His real name was Nicholas James, after his godfather.

"Yeah, Daddy, you 'kay?" TJ asked, as he settled onto the step close to Josh's side.

Josh breathed in a deep breath of fresh air as the sunlight warmed his face and a light June breeze rustled the trees. No bride could have had a better day for her wedding. But that was exactly what Josh had. No bride.

"I'm okay, guys," he assured his boys. "I don't know if you understand what happened in there."

"Nothing happened," TJ griped, tugging at his bow tie. "It was boring."

"Boring," Buzz agreed.

"Oh, it was a little bit exciting," Josh countered. That flurry of nerves as he'd realized he was probably making a mistake, and then the flood of relief when he'd understood that Molly wasn't coming down the aisle… "But you're kind of right about nothing happening. Do you remember what was supposed to happen today?"

As if they were in their preschool classroom, Buzz raised his hand, but he burst out his answer before Josh could "call" on him. "We were s'posed to get married!"

"Stupid!" TJ reached around Josh to poke his brother's back. "Daddy and Molly were s'pose to get married."

"Dummy," Buzz shot back at his brother, "Molly's not here."

Biting his lip to hold back a smile, Josh nodded. "No,

she's not. So I didn't get married." And he hadn't gotten them the stepmother he'd promised them.

"That's okay," Buzz assured his father, patting his shoulder again.

"It's better, just us guys," TJ insisted, jumping to his feet.

Like a jack-in-the-box, Buzz popped up alongside him and declared, "No girls allowed!"

The brothers exchanged another glance, and then TJ asked, "We still gonna move here?"

Josh allowed the smile to take shape then as he stood, too. He wished he were as resilient as his sons. He crouched to their level and pulled them into a close hug. "Yes, we're still moving here," he assured them. Then he whispered, "I bought us a house."

"Really?" Buzz asked, his blue eyes widening.

As he straightened up, Josh nodded. "But don't tell Uncle Nick." He'd deal with his best friend later. Being Nick, he'd probably have a lot to say, in addition to "I told you so," and Josh didn't have the energy to argue with him just then. He hadn't slept at all last night.

"Don't tell Uncle Nick what?" the best man asked as he stepped through the open church door, which Brenna Kelly had been holding with her back. Nick patted his pockets, probably checking to make sure the boys hadn't pilfered any of his valuables.

Josh's attention focused on Brenna, on the color flooding her round face as she was caught eavesdropping on his conversation with the boys. Why did he have the feeling that he might have to deal with her later, too? And why did the thought excite him?

"Nothing," Josh finally said in response to his friend's question.

"We want to ride in the big car, Daddy!" TJ demanded as he clutched Josh's hand and tugged him down the church steps toward the idling black limo.

Buzz grabbed his other hand. His voice softer than his brother's, he asked, "Can we ride in the big car?"

"Please?" TJ added.

Not to be outdone, Buzz echoed the plea, "Please?"

If Josh said no, they'd pitch a fit. Screaming. Kicking. A full-blown temper tantrum. He'd already endured one when he hadn't let them carry the wedding rings down the aisle. In hindsight, he probably should have spared himself that tantrum and let them have the gold bands, instead of insisting his best man carry them. If the twins had flushed the rings, as they'd been known to flush other stuff such as Josh's pager and cell phone—and Nick's, as well—it wouldn't have mattered. Josh hadn't needed the rings after all.

He didn't need the limo, either. But since they'd decided not to cancel the reception, the wedding party might as well take the long black car. "Come on, everyone," he called out to the bridesmaids and groomsmen who filed down the steps behind him. "Let's get in."

"Are you sure?" Brenna Kelly asked, her green gaze intent on his face. He nodded and stepped back so that she and the rest of the wedding party could climb into the stretch limo.

For Brenna's sake he hadn't cancelled the reception. And for her parents' sakes, too—as well as hosting the rehearsal dinner, Emmet and Theresa Kelly had worked hard with the caterer on the wedding feast. Josh owed the older couple a debt of gratitude.

After the rehearsal dinner, the Kellys had had him and the boys stay at their house. They hadn't wanted them to stay with the McClintocks and risk bad luck tied to a wedding superstition involving the groom seeing the bride just before the wedding.

But Josh *had* seen her. She'd walked over to the Kellys' in the middle of the night, where she'd found him sitting alone in the dark on the porch.

"Why'd you ask me to marry you?" she'd asked him.

"I think we can make a marriage work. I think we can be happy," he'd told her, even though he'd been having doubts himself ever since he'd met Brenna Kelly.

She'd sighed, obviously torn. "I'm not sure…"

"Have you changed your mind? Do you want to back out?"

Misery and confusion had darkened her brown eyes. "I don't know."

"We're supposed to be married tomorrow. Do you want to postpone the ceremony?"

"Everyone's worked so hard on it. Brenna, the Kellys, Mrs. George." She'd sighed. "And Clayton has already paid for everything."

"If you've changed your mind, I can reimburse him. I wanted to pay in the first place."

"He won't let you."

Then or *now.* The moment they'd agreed not to cancel the reception, he'd offered—and been rejected. Again.

His mind flipped back to his conversation with Molly. She had sighed and shrugged her shoulders. "I'm probably just experiencing pre-wedding jitters. I'll be fine in the morning."

"If you're not, I will understand," he'd promised. "If you leave me at the altar, or you're standing up there and can't say I do, I *will* understand."

She'd hugged Josh then, and warmth had flooded him,

settling his doubts—and hers, he'd thought. "You're such a *nice* man, Joshua Towers."

He settled alone on the backseat of the limo, the one usually reserved for the groom *and* the bride. *Why was it that nice guys always finished last?*

As the limo pulled away from the church, Molly's kid brother, Rory, asked, "So no one's going to uncork the champagne?"

A disapproving breath hissed out of one of the passengers, and Colleen elbowed her younger brother, who shoved her back. Yet it was Brenna Kelly who landed flat on her butt on the floor, knocked off the end of the long seat she'd shared with Rory, Colleen and Nick. She laughed first, and then everyone else joined in. A chuckle even slipped from Josh's lips.

"What a day…" he mused as he reached down to help her up. When his hand closed around hers, his laughter died as heat tingled in his palm and then shot up his arm.

"It's not over yet," she warned him, her husky voice soft. Her skin was soft, too, but her grip was strong. She rose from the floor, but before she could settle back onto her seat, he tugged her down beside him. He dragged in a deep breath, inhaling the scent of the leather interior mixed with the fragrance from the single lily nestled in her shiny red hair.

Mentally, he kicked himself. His engagement not even officially broken, he had no business being attracted to the maid of honor. Hell, maybe he wasn't such a nice guy after all.

Chapter Two

Brenna stifled a gasp as her hip settled against Josh's hard thigh. He still held her hand, their fingers entwined, until Brenna pulled free. She tried to ease away, but the seat shifted beneath her weight and Josh slid closer. Heat rushed to her face. She couldn't weigh more than he did, not with his height and muscle. Not that she cared—she had long ago made peace with her weight. She would never be model-thin, as Colleen was, or a little pixie, as Abby and Molly were.

She owned a bakery, and she damned well wasn't going to deprive herself of sweets. Or anything else. She should be happy that the reception hadn't been cancelled. She would have a wonderful meal and a huge slice of the chocolate cake with buttercream frosting that her dad had made for Molly. But Brenna wasn't happy. Because Molly wasn't here. *She* should be sitting next to Dr. Towers, not Brenna. And yet Brenna was relieved that Molly wasn't in the limo. She was relieved that her friend hadn't married Josh. And that was why she was unhappy.

How could she wish such humiliation on a nice guy like

Josh? Sure, if Molly hadn't been certain, then she couldn't marry him. But if she'd had doubts, she never should have accepted his proposal. Why had Molly said yes?

Brenna had asked her that question two weeks ago when she'd met Molly for lunch in Grand Rapids, where Molly was going to medical school. But Molly had asked her a question first. "Will you be my maid of honor?"

Brenna had choked on the bite of cheesecake she'd just taken. After clearing her throat with a sip of water, she'd sputtered, "What?"

"I'm getting married," her friend had announced, with none of the excitement Brenna would have expected.

"You and Eric have finally admitted your feelings for each other?" she'd asked, happiness filling her more completely than the creamy dessert had.

"Not Eric." Her usually soft voice had been sharp as Molly stated flatly, "Eric doesn't love me."

Despite all of them knowing better, Molly had always insisted that. "Sure. So if not him, who proposed?"

"Joshua Towers. I met him when I was volunteering at the hospital. He's a cosmetic surgeon. He works with burn victims, especially, and helps repair scars. He's a fine surgeon, and a really great guy. He has the most adorable twin boys, too. He's so sweet and funny."

"How long have you been seeing him?" Because that was the first Brenna had heard about him.

Molly had shrugged. "Not that long. We're both busy, and he's raising the boys on his own. But we really clicked. The first time we went out we talked like old friends, as if we've known each other forever."

"But you haven't, Molly. Why would you accept his proposal so fast?" She hadn't wondered why he would propose. A person couldn't help but love Molly, she was so sweet.

"You'll see when you meet him," Molly had insisted. "And I can't wait for you to meet him, Brenna. You'll love him."

"What about you, Mol? Do *you* love *him?*"

From her friend's blush, Brenna had assumed she had.

A brush of a hand against hers now drew Brenna back to the present and the backseat of the limo.

"Are you okay?" Josh asked softly, his deep voice full of concern.

No wonder Molly had fallen for him. Not only was he movie-star handsome, but he was so kind, too. How could *any* woman not fall for him?

"Me?" She was riddled with guilt because she was infatuated with her best friend's fiancé. No, she wasn't okay. "Why wouldn't I be?"

"You just landed pretty hard on the floor."

She laughed. "Didn't even feel it." She rubbed a hand over her rounded hip. "I have lots of padding."

Josh's gaze slid, like a caress, over her curves. She nearly stopped breathing as he leaned close and murmured, "You're just right."

If he thought she was just right, he must think every other woman in the world was anorexic. No, he was probably lying. The man was a plastic surgeon. How could he look at anyone—and most especially *her*—and not imagine what he might nip, tuck and lipo if he had the chance?

She lowered her voice even more, so that they couldn't be heard above the other conversations taking place in the limo. "The real question is, are *you* okay?"

"Sure," he said, as if dismissing his own feelings.

She reached out and slid her fingers over the back of his hand, offering reassurance and understanding. But her fingers tingled, so she pulled them back and clenched her hand in her lap. To dispel the intimacy between them, she raised her voice as she asked, "Are you sure you want to do this—the limo, the reception?"

"We're not calling it a reception anymore," Josh reminded her. He hadn't gotten married, so he shouldn't feel so guilty about his attraction to her. "It's an open house for the town."

"*We* don't live here," Nick pointed out. "We don't need to go."

"We don't live here *yet*." But as he'd told the boys, Josh had bought a house here. He hadn't had time to share that news with his best friend, though. Since he wouldn't take possession of the house until he got back from his honeymoon, he'd planned on telling Nick then. Like Josh, Nick had only ever lived in cities, and he'd been against starting their private practice in this small town. He certainly wouldn't understand Josh's wanting to move there, too.

"But we're opening our office in Cloverville," Josh said, ignoring his best friend's grimace. "We need to meet our potential patients."

Nick nodded his begrudging agreement.

Rory, bored with the conversation, prodded his older brother. "So, can we open the champagne now?"

Clayton shook his head. "No. And even if we did, you wouldn't get any."

"Come on," Rory whined, sounding a lot like the twins.

The oldest McClintock's voice was gruff with impatience as he began, "Rory…"

The teenager whirled toward Josh. "You're lucky you didn't marry into this family. We never have any fun!"

Buzz and TJ's eyes widened at Rory's belligerent tone. "We had fun last night, Daddy," TJ said.

"At Pop and Mama Kelly's house," Buzz completed his twin's thought.

A grin stole over Josh's mouth. He couldn't help it. Pop and Mama Kelly. They were warm and funny and talked with their hands and insisted everyone call them Pop and Mama. The boys had immediately taken to them, more at ease with them than they were Josh's younger but more reserved parents.

"Why can't we marry the Kellys?" TJ asked.

Next to him, Brenna, as if surprised by the child's question held her breath and tried again to ease away. Josh merely slid closer, unwilling to let her slip away from him as easily as every other woman in his life had done.

Why can't we marry into the Kelly family? he asked himself. With the way in which she'd taken on the responsibility of planning and managing the wedding, he doubted Brenna would accept a man's proposal and then leave him at the altar. And because of that mantle of responsibility that she wore just as easily as the lily in her hair, he doubted she would desert *her* husband and kids.

Still, the one thing Josh had learned from his brief first marriage and even briefer second engagement was that he really had to stop rushing into relationships.

"DR. AND MRS. TOWERS." The words rang in Brenna's ears. Clayton hadn't been able to stop the DJ from introducing the wedding party. No one had been lined up as she'd arranged them at the church, and so almost everyone had been called by the wrong name. But nothing had been quite as wrong as Brenna's walking in next to Josh and being called Mrs. Towers.

Even though she'd had nothing to do with the mistake, embarrassment warmed Brenna's face. It didn't matter that Molly hadn't married Josh today. He still belonged to her. And Brenna's best friend was too smart not to come back eventually and claim her fiancé.

Small, sticky fingers tugged at her hands as the twins sought her attention. "Does this mean you're going to be our new mommy?"

Brenna stared down at their identical faces, their eyes bright with hope. The haircuts were the only way to tell them apart. "Buzz…"

"That man called you Mrs. Towers," TJ said, his voice high with excitement. "Grandma isn't here. She's with Grandpa on a big boat."

Josh had explained that his parents had planned for years to take a cruise on their thirty-fifth anniversary. He hadn't allowed them to cancel the trip, not even for his wedding. He was probably pretty happy now that he hadn't.

"So, then, *you're* Mrs. Towers," Buzz said.

They were so smart for four. But then they'd had to grow up fast since they'd grown up without a mother.

"I'm not really Mrs. Towers," she insisted. "The DJ made a mistake."

"Grandma is the only Mrs. Towers," their father said, leaning down to speak eye-to-eye, man-to-man to his boys. He settled a hand on top of each head, ruffling TJ's moussed-up spikes and smoothing Buzz's fuzz. "But that's okay. We're used to it being just us guys."

Just as when she'd overheard his conversation on the

church steps with his sons, sympathy filled Brenna. How had Josh managed to raise these young boys on his own? Molly had told her how their mother, Josh's first wife, had abandoned him and the boys when the twins were babies. And now Molly had deserted them, too.

"I'm sorry," she murmured, offering an apology for her friend.

Josh, still hunkered down by his sons, lifted his gaze to hers. "I owe *you* the apology," he said. "You worked so hard on this wedding, and it never happened."

She gestured around at the American Legion Hall, which was decorated with red and white fairy lights and balloons and populated by every single townsperson but Molly. And their friend Eric. "It looks like it's happening now. Well, a party is happening now."

"It's not fair this party is for a dumb *girl,*" TJ muttered.

"It was supposed to be *our* party," Buzz chimed in.

Back in the bride's dressing room at the church, everyone had decided to turn the reception into an open house. But the moment Clayton had silenced the embarrassed DJ, Mrs. McClintock had turned the event into a Welcome-Home-Abby-and-Lara-Hamilton party. If not for Molly's wedding, Abby would probably never have returned to the town she couldn't wait to leave eight years before.

Brenna's lips curved into a smile at Mary McClintock's obvious maneuvering. The woman was desperate for Abby, whom she loved like one of her kids, and Lara, whom she loved like a granddaughter, to stay in Cloverville. And of course, she'd probably *really* love it if Abby officially became a McClintock.

Poor Clayton. His mother was a strong woman. She'd had to be in order to survive losing her beloved husband

and she'd fought hard to get what she wanted. Through the crowd Brenna glimpsed the eldest McClintock sibling at the bar. But instead of downing the drink he probably needed, he was writing a check to the bartender.

"*Everyone* can enjoy the party," Brenna assured the boys. Well, everyone but Clayton.

"Thanks to all your hard work planning the reception," Josh said with an appreciative grin. "I'm glad it wasn't cancelled."

Like his wedding. How did he feel about *that* being cancelled? Brenna didn't know him well enough to gauge his mood. He didn't seem angry or even all that hurt. Had having to raise his kids alone, after the devastation of his wife's leaving him, made him an expert at guarding his emotions?

"We want to party, Daddy!" TJ shouted, bored with the adult conversation.

"Party, party!" Buzz echoed.

Josh straightened up, and then stared them down as if a stern look could enforce good behavior. They just grinned at him. As well as missing most of his hair, Buzz was minus a couple of front teeth. Doubting he was old enough for his teeth to have fallen out naturally, Brenna could only imagine the story that accompanied that loss.

"Daddy, we want punch!" TJ shouted.

"Punch, punch!" Buzz echoed.

Brenna smothered a laugh. "I can get them a glass."

"No, hey, let Nick," Josh offered as the best man joined them.

"Let Nick what?" Dr. Jameson asked, his green eyes narrowing. "What else are you going to try talking me into?"

"Getting the boys some punch."

Nick shook his head. "Josh…"

"Hey, five minutes is better than two weeks." Josh turned to Brenna, including her in the conversation with an explanation she would rather not have had. "Nick was supposed to watch the boys while Molly and I were on our honeymoon."

Honeymoon. Her stomach lurched at the thought of Molly and Josh on their honeymoon. Making love. Her best friend and the man she… Nothing. She could feel *nothing* for Dr. Joshua Towers.

"Punch, punch, Uncle Nick," Buzz demanded as he latched on to the handsome doctor's leg.

"We need to talk," Nick murmured to Josh as he let the twins drag him away.

"Don't drink too much and spoil your appetites," Brenna called after the boys. "We'll be eating soon." Alone with Josh, in spite of the crowded hall, her nerves jangled. "I should really go and see if my folks and Mrs. George need any help with the food."

Before she could slip away, Josh caught her hand and squeezed her fingers. "I never really thanked you for all that you've done."

Her lips parted, a nervous breath escaping. *Damn.* She ran a business, for crying out loud. She'd run this wedding before it had all fallen apart. It would take more than blue eyes and a killer grin to addle her brain and make her forget her loyalty to a friend.

"I didn't mind. Molly is my best friend," she reminded him—and herself. Not only had Molly been her friend since kindergarten, she'd been her college roommate when they'd both left Cloverville for the first time. If not for Molly, Brenna probably would have been too homesick to stick out college for her bachelor's degree, let alone for an MBA.

She sighed. "I just wish things had turned out differently."

Dr. and Mrs. Towers. The announcement echoed in her mind, reminding her that for a brief moment he'd belonged to *her* and not Molly. But the DJ had been wrong, and so was she. She couldn't betray her friendship with Molly— not even for a man such as Josh.

"Now that I think about it," Josh mused, his eyes twinkling, "isn't a maid of honor like a second? If the bride can't honor her commitment, her maid of honor has to step in?"

"You're confusing a wedding with a duel," she retorted. "No wonder Molly went out the window."

Josh laughed, amused more by the expression on her beautiful face, the mock horror widening her green eyes, than by her accusation. "You forget that I've been married already. From experience, I can assure you that it's pretty easy to confuse a duel and a marriage."

Amy had picked endless fights in order to get what she wanted. And in the end that hadn't included her children or her husband. She'd wanted her freedom more.

"I'm sorry," Brenna said again, her eyes tender with sympathy over the thought of the boys' mother abandoning them. "Molly told me that your wife left when the twins were babies."

He shrugged off the memories of frustration and fear— could he manage alone? "It was a good thing, really, that she left when they were so young. They don't remember her, so they can't miss her."

"I'm sorry," she said again.

"It's my fault," Josh volunteered. "She was young, and I should have realized she was too young to become a wife and mother. My long hours at the hospital, having twins—it was too much for her. I can't blame her for being overwhelmed."

"That's no excuse for leaving her husband and children." Brenna's voice hardened with indignation as she proclaimed, even though she'd never met his ex-wife, "She's clearly a fool."

He grinned at the remark. "Maybe you should have been my best man."

Her face softened as she returned his smile. "Why?"

"Nick called *me* the fool."

"Some friend," she scoffed.

"My thoughts exactly." But Josh knew that Nick *was* a good friend. His best friend. As well as always being honest with him, more often than not the bastard was also right. He'd thought Josh crazy for rushing into his relationships with Amy and Molly. Josh should have listened to him both times. He had to stop rushing into things. He had to fight this attraction to Brenna.

THE GROOM STOOD ALONE atop the five-tier wedding cake, which was bedecked with red and white frosting flowers. In his plastic tux and with his painted-on smile, he looked quite happy. Certainly not like a man who'd been left at the altar. But as with Josh, this groom's bride also was missing.

A big hand slapped Josh's shoulder, causing him to stumble forward. Grabbing the edge of the table, he caught himself from falling headfirst into frosting. The tiers jiggled, and the lone groom wobbled on the top. But he didn't fall down.

"Sorry, boy, so sorry," offered Emmet "Pop" Kelly, his strong fingers grasping Josh's shoulder.

Mr. Kelly was a mammoth man with burly arms and a bulging belly that started just below his neck. Despite the

lines of age on his face, his hair was still black—all but for
one shock of white that fell across his brow. "Mr. Kelly…"

"Pop. I told you everyone calls me Pop."

"Pop…"

"Damn shame, boy, about the bride. I can't figure out
what happened to her. She was just gone."

"She left a note," Josh explained. "She needs some
time to think…"

"No, not *your* bride. His." He pointed toward the plastic
groom. "I swear she was on the cake when it left the bakery.
I loaded it into the truck myself. Well, that nice kid helped
me—Harold's nephew."

A headache pounded at Josh's temple. While he'd fallen
for the whole town of Cloverville the minute he'd set foot
into it, he would need to live there a while before he'd be
able to catch up on who was related to whom and who lived
where and what used to be located in some spot before
weather, age or redevelopment had brought it down. Hell,
he might never catch up. Even so, the first time he'd come
to Cloverville, he'd realized that it would be the perfect
place to raise his boys, and that had been *before* he'd met
Brenna Kelly.

His eyes narrowed as he glanced again at the lonely
plastic groom. *Could they have…* Spying small finger-
prints in the frosting on the bottom tier, he asked, "Have
you seen Buzz and TJ?"

The older man laughed, his eyes crinkling at the corners.
"The boys have been having a great time."

At least someone was, then. Josh had barely been able
to eat for all the townspeople staring at him and casting him
sympathetic glances. Mrs. McClintock turning the event
into a welcome-home party for Abby and Lara had taken

some of the attention away from him. Before he'd met them, Molly had filled him in on all her friends. Eight years earlier Abby had left Cloverville in disgrace, but apparently the town had forgiven her her transgressions because now they genuinely welcomed her back. Well, everyone but Clayton.

And the town had welcomed Josh and his boys, as well. Even though Molly had backed out of marrying him, Josh couldn't back out of moving there. He'd been right to believe this town was the perfect place to raise his boys.

"When did you see them last? And where?" he asked Pop. "They weren't heading to the bathroom?" With a little plastic bride. He patted the pockets of his tux and breathed a sigh of relief. At least they didn't have his cell phone. Or his pager. Or his wallet. But, man, if that bride had a train on her plastic dress, they could clog the whole plumbing system of the American Legion Hall.

Dark paneling showed through the thin coat of white paint on the walls, and underfoot the linoleum was worn and cracked with age. His ex-wife would have hated this place. He'd had to book a swanky hotel in Grand Rapids for their small wedding. But with white and red lights and balloons, Brenna had transformed the dark hall, the only place in town for a reception, so that it was as enchanting as…she was.

As the older man rambled on, Josh scanned the hall. He should have been searching for his mischievous boys, but instead his gaze locked on Brenna. In her red satin gown, with her hair flowing around her shoulders and her pale skin shimmering with the glow from the fairy lights, she looked like a princess. Not like one from the old fables, which Buzz and TJ had grown bored with long ago, but one from the hormone-fuelled dreams of a teenage boy. Something about Brenna Kelly brought Josh back to that time before med school, before marriage, before kids, when life had been simpler—when his breath had caught and his pulse had raced at the mere sight of a pretty girl.

Brenna turned, and across the hall, their gazes met. Her lips, nearly as red as her gown, lifted in a smile. And Josh's breath caught. And his pulse raced.

"Son?"

"Yeah," Josh, distracted, responded to the older man.

"So it's settled then." The old man clapped his meaty hands together. "I'll tell Mama. She'll be thrilled."

"Huh?" Josh pulled his attention away from the daughter to concentrate on her father. "What?"

"Mama was already fretting that she didn't have enough time with the boys," Pop elaborated. "They bring so much energy and life to the old house."

"I'm sorry." Josh shook his head. "I don't understand…"

"Well, if Molly just needs time, you'll want to wait for her. She's a smart girl, nose always in a book. She'll figure things out quickly," Pop said.

Josh knew Molly had already figured out one thing— that she didn't want him. When she turned up again, he doubted it would be to marry *him*. "Mr.…Pop…"

"Despite all the development on the east side of town, Cloverville still doesn't have a hotel or motel. So you'll stay with us," the older man concluded.

Spend more time in close proximity to Brenna Kelly? He couldn't. He shook his head. "You're generous to open up your home to me and my sons, but I can't impose," he insisted. "You've already done too much."

Pop's meaty hand smacked Josh's shoulder. "Nonsense. The house is too big for just us and Brenna."

Josh couldn't argue with him. The old Victorian house, with its turret and wide wraparound porch, was huge, but the Kellys had done their best to fill it to the rafters with antiques. *Breakables* had been his first thought when he'd seen their home initially the day before. The boys had thought it a gingerbread house, with its bright yellow siding and teal-and-purple trim. He'd had to watch them to make sure they didn't try to break off a corner in order to taste it.

"Your house is beautiful," Josh complimented the older man, "and full of lovely treasures. I adore my boys, but they're not very careful with fragile things. I'd hate it if they broke one of your collectibles. Really, we're better off going back to Grand Rapids for the moment."

And he'd be better off away from Brenna and temptation.

Pop laughed. "That junk? Mama and I inherited most of it from our families. We don't have much left now."

"Family?" Josh asked.

The old man nodded, his eyes glistening.

"You have all those keepsakes to remember them by." Josh offered comfort, he hoped, to his new friend. "And that's all the more reason not to trust my boys around your heirlooms."

"You don't remember people with *stuff,*" Pop scoffed. "You remember them with your mind. So don't worry about our junk. Your boys can't hurt a thing."

Josh's cell phone company sure hadn't agreed with that. Neither had any of the twins' nannies. Stumped for another excuse, he said, "If you're sure you have room…"

Despite the size of the house, there were only three bedrooms. He'd spent the night on a foldout bed in the parlor.

"Even with all our belongings, there's plenty of room. Mama and I are usually rattling around all alone in the house since Brenna's either at the bakery or traveling for the business," her father explained. "She came home from college just bursting with ideas to expand the bakery. She built onto the back of the building and hired a slew of people. So Mama and I stay in the kitchen now and let her manage the rest. She's got Kelly Confections in nearly every grocery store in the country now. That girl thrives on being in charge."

"Does she know that you've made this offer?"

Pop sighed. "No, so she'll probably be upset."

Josh turned toward her again, but she wasn't standing where she'd been on the other side of the room anymore. Although he scanned the crowd carefully, he couldn't spot her. "I don't want to upset Brenna." That was the last thing he wanted to do, after everything she'd done for him.

"You won't. I have." Her dad laughed. "She'll be mad that I beat her to the offer. She'll love having you and the boys stay with us."

"We won't stay long," he assured the other man—and himself. Even though Molly hadn't become his wife, she was a friend and he'd like to make sure she was all right.

"You're staying?" a throaty feminine voice asked.

He'd lost sight of Brenna Kelly because she'd come up behind him. He turned toward her and nodded. "Your father invited me, Buzz and TJ to stay with you."

"Pop?" she questioned, her eyes widening as she stared at her dad.

Her father ignored her question and asked, "Honey, did Mama fetch my knife yet?"

Josh's stomach tightened. "Knife?" Maybe the old man had noticed him ogling his daughter.

"To cut the cake, boy," Pop explained, with another

smack on Josh's back. "I better see what's keeping that woman," he grumbled as he walked off. "She's probably fixing her hair, as if she could get any prettier…"

Her daughter certainly couldn't. Josh dragged in a deep breath, bracing himself for more time spent with Brenna. He'd been crazy to accept her father's invitation. He couldn't stay with her—and not fall for her.

Chapter Three

Left alone with her houseguest, Brenna could only stare up at the jilted groom. The one on the cake. She couldn't look at Josh and manage to think. "Pop's really upset about the bride."

"Yeah, I know."

"Mama wanted the bakery to carry the one-piece groom-and-bride cake toppers, but Pop insisted they be individual so that we can mix and match, you know," she rambled uncharacteristically, at the mercy of her nerves. "Brunette to brunette or brunette to blonde…"

"Or brunette to redhead," Josh teased.

Heat rushed to Brenna's face as his flirty tone flustered her. "Yeah, well, we don't carry that many redheads. Not much demand."

"Then I guess I'm not the only fool."

"What?" she asked, totally confused by the comment and the twinkle in his striking blue eyes.

"I can't understand there not being a *great* demand for redheads." He grinned.

"Pop blames it on our notorious temper, you know." While she didn't have much of a temper, she'd rather blame the lack of demand for her on that than on her weight. She wasn't about to starve herself into a size six, or she *would* have a hair-trigger temper and an ornery disposition. She knew from experience.

In her teens, during the rage of crash diets, she'd nearly lost her friends instead of losing any weight. But they'd remained loyal and supportive, no matter how bitchy she'd been. She had to be loyal and supportive, too—especially of Molly.

"Pop warned me that you might be mad," Josh shared.

Had her father picked up on her feelings? "He thought I'd be mad that you and Buzz and TJ are staying with us?"

"That he asked me first." Josh sighed. "But I can see that's not the case. If you'd rather I find someplace else to stay…"

Her heart skipped. "Does this mean you're still going to stay in Cloverville?"

"Nick and I are building an office here," he reminded her. "We're starting our private practice here."

"You haven't changed your mind…?" When Molly had told her of his plans, she hadn't understood why an orthopedic surgeon and a plastic surgeon would start a practice in Cloverville. Although the town was growing, she couldn't imagine there being much demand for their services.

"Nick would love it if I did," Josh admitted. "He's not thrilled about my choice of location for our venture. But it's not that far from the hospital where we have privileges—just a little over an hour away. And when Molly told me your town doctor had retired, I saw an opportunity here."

Brenna thought she knew what he'd seen in Cloverville—a life with Molly. "So you're going to handle more than just your specialties?"

He nodded. "Yes. I am. I'm going to hire a physician's assistant, and Nick wants to bring in a physical therapist, too."

Although he might have rushed his proposal to Molly, Josh apparently had given more time and consideration to the plans for his practice. Brenna could appreciate a man with a brain for business.

"And I bought a house here," he continued.

"You bought a house?" He wasn't just going to work in Cloverville, he was going to live here, as well?

"I don't have possession of it yet," he explained. "At closing the sellers and I agreed they wouldn't have to move out for two more weeks."

"After your…" she almost choked on the word "…honeymoon? Does Molly know?"

"About the house?" He shook his head. "I was going to tell her tonight."

"The house was her wedding present," Brenna realized. "You were going to surprise her."

Sure, some women might have considered his buying a house without his bride's input to be high-handed. Ordinarily Brenna would be one of those women. But this was Josh, and for some reason his doing it didn't make him seem chauvinistic, just incredibly romantic. Jealousy churned in her stomach, but she settled it with a sigh. "And instead *she* surprised *you*."

"Brenna…"

"So you're going to stay with us for two weeks?" She drew in a deep breath, but the pressure on her chest wouldn't allow her lungs to expand. "Or are you going to go on your honeymoon anyway?"

"Bermuda alone?" he said with a wry laugh. "Now that would be sad. Do you want to join me?"

"Josh…"

The sparkle in his eyes clued her in to the joke. "You're the second, remember? Gotta take up the sword for the bride."

She shook her head. "There's a reason Pop didn't ask me to fetch his knife. I'd cut myself."

Not to mention the fact that her heart would bleed if she fell for a man such as Josh Towers, a man who must still long for another woman. Her best friend. No, she didn't intend to be anyone's second. Not even his…

"I NEED TO TALK TO MOLLY," Brenna stated her demand into the cell phone pressed to her ear as she paced the alley behind the American Legion Hall. She needed Molly to come home and reclaim her groom, before Brenna did something stupid like trying to claim him for herself.

Eric's deep voice vibrated in the phone. "Bren, I told you the first couple of times you called that she isn't here."

So even though she'd called his cell this time, he was home at the small cabin on the fishing lake just outside of Cloverville. Perhaps Brenna should have just driven over…

"You told me, but should I believe you?" This was Eric, and everyone in Cloverville but Molly knew how he felt about her. "Eric, you'd lie for Molly. We all know you'd do anything she asked you to do."

"We're friends," he said, as if that explained everything. "That's what friends do."

"She asked you to be in her wedding party, but you backed out," she reminded him. Pulling out at the last moment had messed up the wedding party so that Clayton had had to pull double duty, walking Abby down the aisle and then going back to give away the bride.

"So why would you think I'd lie for her?"

Brenna, hearing the smirk in his voice, smothered a scream of frustration. Like the younger brother she'd never had, Eric had always enjoyed teasing her. But not in the way Josh teased her. Josh's teasing felt different—made her feel different.

"Eric," she said, lowering her voice in a way she hoped would seem threatening. She didn't care that he'd grown—considerably—from the puny, little kid he'd once been. She was mad enough to win a wrestling match with the ex-Marine anyway. "Make her come to the phone, or I'm coming over there. Now. I have to talk to her."

Eric's laugh echoed in the cell. "God, Bren, you're still just as bossy as when we were kids. Still the spoiled only child who's used to getting her way."

He was an only child, too. And so was Abby Hamilton. Brenna could have pointed that out, but Eric was right. She was the only spoiled one in their group, the one with the doting parents who'd given her everything she'd ever wanted. But she had yet to give Pop and Mama what they really wanted—grandchildren. Maybe that was why they'd invited Josh and the boys to stay longer. They wanted as much time as they could manage with Buzz and TJ.

Maybe if they'd been able to have more kids, they wouldn't have been in such a hurry for grandkids now. As it was they hadn't been able to conceive Brenna until they'd been in their forties. If they were younger, maybe they'd be willing to wait until she was ready to settle down and had the time to find a guy who didn't already belong to someone else.

Just the way the house she wanted now belonged to someone else.

When Molly had announced her engagement, Brenna had taken a hard look at her own life. She'd thought Molly would be the last of their friends to marry—she'd been so focused on becoming a doctor that she hadn't even dated in college. But here was Molly, engaged, and Abby, a mother, while Brenna still lived at home with her parents. She'd decided then to start spending some time on her personal life, and so she'd gone house hunting. But the house she'd fallen in love with had sold to someone else before Brenna could even put in a bid.

"Bren, you still there?" Eric's voice rumbled through the phone. "I'm just kidding. You know I love you…"

But not the way he loved Molly. Brenna smiled. "If you loved me, you'd let me talk to her."

"Bren…"

"Eric, she chose *me* as her maid of honor." Probably only because Eric wouldn't have looked all that good in a dress. "And she's left *me* with this disaster."

A door opened from the Legion Hall, and music and laughter spilled into the alley. Maybe the reception wasn't a disaster. But everything else was. Her feelings for the jilted groom, for example. She shouldn't be so fascinated— or was that infatuated?—with Josh.

"She left a note, too, asking for some time alone to figure things out," Eric reminded her. "A good friend would give her that time."

"You know about the note." Molly was there, probably standing right next to him, listening in on Brenna's call.

"Colleen or Abby must have told me," he explained. "They've been calling, too. Wanting to make sure she's all right. But you don't seem as concerned about Molly as you do about someone else."

Josh.

"I *am* worried about Molly." Because she'd obviously lost her mind. Why else would she have left Dr. Joshua Towers at the altar?

"You don't need to worry," Eric assured her before hanging up. "She just needs some time alone. Then she'll be all right."

But would Brenna be okay? If Molly stayed away and Brenna had Joshua Towers in her house, all to herself, would she survive with her heart intact? She doubted it. Still, she wouldn't have him all to herself. No woman would. She'd have his sons, too.

From the other side of the Dumpster drifted the excited chatter and giggles of two little boys. Brenna crept around the large metal container, ducking as a spray of pop arced toward her like a liquid rainbow. While most of the cola ran in rivulets down the corner of the Dumpster near Brenna's head, a few drops caught her face, one sliding down her cheek to drip from her chin. She turned toward the boys, meeting two pairs of blue eyes that widened in astonishment and fear. They hadn't meant to hit her.

Brenna sank her teeth into her bottom lip, keeping herself from smiling. She cleared her throat to stifle a laugh and admonished them, "Nicholas James! Thomas Joshua!"

"You know our real names?" TJ asked, his voice quavering with nerves and surprise.

Brenna had overheard Josh calling them by their full names when he'd been trying to get them to settle down in the guestroom the night before. Now, through the wall of her room, she'd have to listen to him—every night for two weeks?—reading bedtime stories to his sons. But it was better that they, and not their father, slept in the room next to hers. Or Brenna wouldn't be able to sleep at all, for his being so tantalizingly close.

The twins exchanged a glance. Then Buzz twisted his lips, speaking out of the side of his mouth to his brother. "We're in trouble now."

They weren't the only ones.

Brenna continued to hold in a laugh as she took in their condition. TJ's spiky hair dripped cola onto his face and the shoulders of his saturated tuxedo jacket. Buzz blinked pop from his eyelashes—it streamed down his cheeks like tears, and then trickled along the pleats of his once-white shirt. "We need to get you two cleaned up before your father sees you."

Josh had enough on his mind with his missing bride, plus he was probably going crazy looking for his boys. He didn't need to find them like this. As it was, he certainly wasn't going to get his deposit back on their matching tuxedos.

"Okay, guys, let's go," she ordered, herding them back into the hall.

They balked at the door to the ladies' room, as if Brenna were trying to drag them into a dentist's chair for a root canal.

"We're not going in there," TJ insisted.

"We're boys," Buzz pointed out, as if she hadn't noticed.

"We need to use the *men's* room," TJ explained.

"*I* can't go in *there*," Brenna replied. "And since I just saw your dad and Uncle Nick go into the men's room, I think you'd rather use the lad—"

Buzz and TJ hurled their bodies against the door in their haste to scramble into the other restroom and away from their father. Brenna caught the door before it swung back in her face and followed them into the empty room. Fortunately, everyone was on the dance floor, shaking their bodies and singing along with a classic Bob Seger song. Brenna hummed a few bars as the twins shucked their jackets and cummerbunds. TJ got his tie caught around his head, the bow planted in the middle of his forehead.

Laughing, Buzz dropped to his knees on the green-tiled floor and pointed at his brother. "You're a girl. You're a little sissy girl."

TJ slammed his hands against his brother's sodden shirt-front. "*You're* a sissy girl."

"You're a sissy girl!"

"No one's a sissy girl," Brenna insisted as she turned on the water tap and reached for the paper towels that were folded in a basket on the Formica counter.

"*You're* a girl." The boys turned on her, as if her gender was a dirty word. TJ tugged the bow tie over his head, and Buzz rose to his feet.

"But I'm no sissy," Brenna warned them as she cupped the flow from the faucet and sprayed water all over the twins.

They squealed but they didn't run, catching water in their open mouths and letting it drip from their chins.

She stopped spraying them, in order to mop them up with wet and then dry towels. "At least you didn't have punch." She could just imagine the bright red stains on their clothes.

"Uncle Nick said it had nails in it."

"Spikes," Buzz corrected his brother. "Uncle Nick said someone put spikes in it."

"Someone spiked the punch?" Brenna asked. Obviously the boys hadn't had any, as their little bodies fairly hummed with energy from a pure caffeine high.

"Who'd put spikes in punch?" TJ asked, wrinkling his nose as Brenna wiped off his face.

"Rory," she muttered. Since the boy had hit his teens,

poor Mrs. McClintock had been struggling to keep her youngest on the straight and narrow. Even though Mary McClintock had been a single mom since her husband died, she had always had help from her other offspring. Especially Clayton, the eldest and most responsible of the McClintocks.

What about Josh—who did he have? His parents hadn't bothered coming to his wedding, which Brenna felt should have taken priority over their anniversary, and while the twins called his best friend Uncle Nick, he wasn't really their uncle. He certainly wasn't maternal. The boys needed a mother.

Buzz shivered in his damp shirt. "I'm cold, Brenna."

"You're a sissy girl," TJ accused his brother through quivering lips. He struggled to keep his teeth from chattering when gusts of cool air blew out of the vents above them.

Hunkering down beside the boys, Brenna wrapped an arm around each twin and pulled them close for a hug.

"Umm-hmm," Buzz nodded, before he and TJ wriggled loose. "You smell good."

"You're really pretty, too," TJ said, probably in competition with his twin for the better compliment. His sticky fingers tugged on a lock of her hair. "I like red. It's my favorite color."

TJ's father had said it was his favorite color, too, which was why she'd chosen it for the flowers and the bridesmaids' dresses.

"I wish you were going to be our new mommy," the boy said, easily winning the compliment competition.

"We like you more than Molly," Buzz agreed. "Why can't you be our new mommy?"

"Uh…" she stammered, having no idea what to say. "Your daddy and I haven't even known each other very long."

"He doesn't know Molly, either," TJ pointed out.

They were so smart.

"But he doesn't love me, honey." And Brenna, growing up with parents who were as devoted to each other as they were to her, had vowed long ago to marry for *nothing* less than love.

"He doesn't love Molly, either," Buzz insisted.

"Honey, your dad wouldn't have asked her to marry him if he didn't love her." Would he have? Or was he just as desperate to find a mother for his sons as they were? "Besides which, you guys don't really know me."

"We love you," TJ declared.

Brenna blinked back tears of longing. She didn't have to worry about just falling for Josh. She was falling for his sons, too.

BRENNA MOVED through the crowd, looking for Josh. If not for Nick just telling her he was still looking for the boys, she wouldn't have sought him out. She would have gone on trying to avoid him. And his sons.

She found him near the bar, cornered by two of the town's busiest bodies. Mrs. Hild, the organist, stood so close to him that the brim of her flower-trimmed hat poked into his chest. "It's such a scandal."

"A real scandal," her cohort, Mrs. Carpenter, whole-heartedly agreed, patting her home-permed white curls. Her husband, the owner of Carpenter's Hardware on Main Street, had the well-earned reputation of being the thrifti-est man in town.

"I can't believe Molly would run out like that on her own wedding." The flowers wobbled as Mrs. Hild shook her head. "Now it's the wedding-that-wasn't."

"Doesn't make sense," Mrs. Carpenter agreed. "Molly has always been such a smart girl."

"Nose always in a book," Mrs. Hild added. "Read every-thing in the library. Heck, she just about lived in that library."

"Makes no sense," Mrs. Carpenter repeated, her eyes wide as she assessed Josh's good looks.

"Can I borrow Dr. Towers?" Brenna asked, reaching between the older women to grasp Josh's arm and pull him away. "Your children need you."

"Such adorable little scamps," Mrs. Carpenter murmured as Brenna led him from the bar.

"And their father." Mrs. Hild's loud sigh reached them. "He's the spitting image of JFK junior. Such a handsome, handsome boy…"

"Molly McClintock must have lost her mind," Mrs. Carpenter declared.

Brenna swallowed her agreement, along with a chuckle at the lasciviousness of the two women.

"Where are the boys? I've been looking all over for them," Josh said, his eyes dark with concern for his children. He obviously didn't care what Mrs. Hild, Mrs. Carpenter or anyone else said about him. Or he wouldn't have shown up at his reception.

"Evidently you haven't looked in the alley," Brenna informed him. "Or the ladies' room."

He closed his eyes. "They were outside? By themselves?"

"I was with them every minute," she assured him, although she hadn't been quite fast enough to prevent the pop fight.

"And the ladies' room?" he asked. "Are the toilets working?"

Brenna laughed. "Yes. Everything's okay. You probably won't get the deposit back on their tuxedoes. But otherwise they're fine."

He pushed a hand through his black hair as a grin stole

across his mouth. "Never a dull moment. Not since the day they were born. They need constant supervision, or they get into trouble. Where are they now?"

"With my folks. Mama and Pop can handle them," she assured him. "Nick said you were looking for them, though."

"Where is he?"

"Are you still avoiding your best man?" she asked.

Josh shook his head. Just as the town gossips had cornered him at the bar, Nick had cornered Josh in the men's room earlier. His friend didn't understand why Josh had insisted on coming to the reception. Hell, he didn't understand why Josh hadn't changed his mind about opening the office and moving to Cloverville. He expected Josh to sell the building and the house he'd finally admitted to buying. He hadn't realized what Josh already understood— that Cloverville had a lot to offer.

"Dance with me," he said. "I haven't danced once tonight."

She shook her head. "I just rescued you from the town busybodies, but you're determined to get their tongues wagging again."

Josh shrugged. "Sweetheart, I'm going to be the talk of this town for many years to come, no matter what I do." Maybe Nick was right. Maybe he *should* change his plans, sell the office building, sell the house and salvage some of his pride. "Why is dancing with you going to get the tongues wagging again?"

Her usually throaty voice slightly prim, she informed him, "A groom is supposed to dance his first dance with the bride."

"That's a little hard to do when the bride's taken off," Josh pointed out. "Pretty sad that a woman was so desperate to get away from me that she ran away from all her family and friends, too."

"Maybe not all her friends," Brenna muttered.

"What?" Was Brenna referring to the guy who'd backed out of the wedding party at the last minute—the guy Molly had often talked about, Eric South? Although South was a paramedic at the hospital where Josh worked, he couldn't remember ever having met him. Of course he didn't often work out of the E.R. "Do you know where she is?"

"Sure, I'll dance with you," she said now, as if desperate to change the subject.

Josh wouldn't pressure her for Molly's whereabouts in the way that Nick would. His best man thought Josh needed to talk to his fiancée, in order to accept that the engagement was over. But even though their engagement wasn't officially broken, Josh knew he and Molly wouldn't ever be getting married.

He linked his fingers with Brenna's and led her through the twirling and swaying couples on the dance floor. "Now I see where Nick's gotten to. He's dancing with Colleen," he observed. He had known Nick a long time, but he couldn't remember if he'd ever seen that particular expression on his friend's face before—a mixture of awe, fear and fascination.

"And Abby and Clayton are dancing," Brenna mused breathlessly, obviously stunned at this new development between her friends.

Finding an open space on the floor, Josh stopped and turned toward Brenna. But he didn't have her attention, as she still watched the other couple. Brenna's eyes widened as the oldest McClintock leaned over and kissed Abby.

"Wow," she whistled, "no wonder the boys were cold. Hell has just frozen over."

Josh pulled Brenna's soft, curvy body into his arms. "The boys were cold?"

He closed his eyes on a wave of guilt. He should be focused on them right now, on their disappointment in not getting the new mommy he'd promised them. Instead he was focusing only on Brenna, on how perfectly she fit into his arms, against his body. How his pulse raced and his skin tingled from the slightest contact with her.

"I warmed them up," she assured him, "with some dry paper towels and a hug."

"Buzz and TJ?" he checked.

"I haven't noticed any other miniature versions of you running around here," she teased.

"They stood still long enough for you to give them a hug?" he asked, disbelieving. He had to bribe them for hugs.

"Well, they were cold from their pop fight."

He winced. "Pop fight?" No wonder she considered the tuxedo deposits a loss.

"They were shaking up pop bottles, then spraying them at each other like squirt guns."

Josh groaned. "I'm sorry they've been so much trouble."

"*They're* no trouble at all."

"But I am?" Josh asked, surprised by her tone. Did she feel it, too—the attraction, the possibilities between them?

Chapter Four

Brenna dragged in a breath, scented with Josh's citrusy aftershave, and shook her head. "You're no trouble."

His arms tightened around her back, pulling her closer so that her breasts pressed against his chest. His heart pounded fast and hard—she could feel the beat of it in sync with hers. He said, "You don't sound convinced."

"That's not what I meant."

"Of course not," he agreed, easing away slightly. "I've been nothing but trouble for you. You worked so hard on the wedding and reception."

Brenna glanced toward her friends, all of whom had abandoned their partners on the dance floor. She gave Colleen credit for leaving the best man standing alone. Nick Jameson was obviously trouble, and Colleen had realized it. The girl was stronger than she knew. Pride lifted Brenna's lips into a smile. Colleen was nearly as much her little sister as she was Molly's. She had often hung out at the Kelly house growing up, and she still did today.

And Clayton. The man looked as stunned to have kissed Abby as Brenna had been to witness it. Even though Abby had run away from him, maybe she'd finally stopped fighting her feelings. Mrs. McClintock might get her wish after all.

"Maybe it's not turning out so badly," Brenna said, referring to his earlier comment. Then her breath caught as she thought about how this sounded. "I mean, for everyone else. Obviously it hasn't worked out for you."

"Brenna…" He slid his fingertips along her cheekbone to the curve of her jaw. Her skin tingled everywhere he touched her.

His eyes darkening as his pupils widened, he murmured, "Maybe it's not turning out so badly for me, either." Then he leaned forward, as if he intended to kiss her.

Her heart pounding wildly, Brenna pulled away. She wanted Josh so badly she must have imagined he felt the attraction, too. And that just wasn't possible. "I really need to go check on my friends."

Abby kissing Clayton. Colleen staring up at Nick Jameson as if she were deeply infatuated. Apparently, Brenna wasn't the only one who was falling.

Josh nodded. "I understand. I wish…"

"What?" She couldn't stop herself from asking.

He shook his head. "I wish that I was your friend, too." The sparkle in his eyes hinted that maybe he would like to be more than her friend. But she had to be imagining that, just as she'd imagined he intended to kiss her. That sparkle must have been a reflection from the strobe light spinning over their heads.

"We are friends," she assured him. With his first e-mail, she'd felt as if they'd become friends, as if she were planning Molly's wedding more for Joshua Towers than for the friend Brenna had known since kindergarten.

And now she was ashamed of herself. Could she be any

more disloyal? Yes—she could have kissed her best friend's groom.

"I really need to check on my friends," she insisted, her voice cracking with nerves.

"And I should go check on the boys," he murmured as he followed her off the dance floor.

Brenna picked up her pace, dodging other couples and dancing children. She needed some distance between them, needed to gain some perspective.

She'd already lied to Josh when she'd assured him he wasn't trouble. Because he was—for Brenna's head *and* her heart. How would she survive two weeks with him and his lovable boys living in her house?

JOSH STRIPPED OFF his bow tie and shrugged out of his jacket, then draped it over the back of one of the spindly-legged chairs in the parlor. He shouldn't have agreed to stay here, for so many reasons.

His body tensed as the floorboards creaked above his head. Brenna's room was directly above the parlor, in the turret of the Kellys' old Victorian house. She was awake, too. Her parents had come home a while ago, checked in on him and then headed to bed. And the boys were dead to the world, sleeping just as they played—flat out. There was something intimate, he thought, about Brenna and him being the only two people awake in a quiet house.

He shook his head. There could be *nothing* intimate between them, no matter how much Brenna's beauty and generosity tempted him. He was still engaged. And even if he wasn't, he was done rushing into relationships.

Something beeped in the small, crowded room. Did the Kellys have a lie detector among their antiques? But then he realized that the sound emanated from his jacket. He pulled his cell phone, which issued a low-battery warning, from one of the pockets. When he flipped it open the little envelope icon flashed on the LCD screen, indicating voice mail.

"Probably Nick," he muttered. He had an excuse for deleting the message, too—his battery was low. But he still appreciated his friend's concern, so he speed-dialed the voice-mail box and punched in his access code.

A soft, feminine voice filled his ear. "Josh, I'm so sorry. Please don't hate me…"

How could he? When he suspected she'd saved them both from making a terrible mistake.

Molly's message continued, "You said you'd understand. I hope you do."

That was it, and the phone reverted to an automated voice telling him which number to push to delete the message and which to save.

"Molly, what do I do?" he asked himself, trying to decipher her cryptic message. "Do I delete or save?" Were they over, was their engagement broken, or would she return and expect him to be waiting?

He'd never said he loved her, and she'd never made that vow to him. They cared for each other, though. And yet she must have realized just in time that that wasn't enough to build a marriage on. If only he'd realized that before he'd proposed.

Undoing some of the buttons on his shirt, he struggled to compose himself. Heavy velvet drapes hung at the parlor windows and furniture filled every corner. Feeling trapped in the crowded room and by his own promise, he ducked out onto the porch.

A shadow shifted near the railing where the porch

wrapped around the kitchen and dining room. Maybe he and Brenna weren't the only two awake.

"Pop?" he called out as he skirted rockers and deck chairs until he reached the table where someone sat.

Then the clouds shifted, and moonlight shone so brightly it could have been morning already. He glanced at his watch. Hell, it nearly was. His breath caught as he realized who else occupied the deck. Brenna sat at the patio table. Moonlight shimmered in her hair, making the auburn strands glow like fire. She'd changed out of her bridesmaid dress, and now the tank top she wore with pajamas bottoms left her creamy shoulders bare but for thin spaghetti straps. He let go of the breath he'd been holding.

"Want some?" she asked in that husky voice of hers.

"What?"

She lifted a fork. "Cake?"

"No." He shook his head and lied. "I'm not hungry." Then he swallowed, as nervous as a teenager on his first date, and added, "I'm still full from dinner." Even though he hadn't eaten more than a few bites.

"There's always room for cake," she insisted.

"Sounds like something Buzz and TJ would say," he remarked, debating whether he should pull out the chair beside her or return to the parlor.

Her mouth curved into an affectionate smile. "I just knew they were kindred spirits."

"Well, they've been called little devils," he admitted.

"They're sweet."

"When they're sleeping."

"Why aren't *you* sleeping?" Then she winced and answered her own question. "The pullout bed probably isn't very comfortable."

"It's fine."

"You should have taken my bed, and then you'd be right next to the boys."

"I can't take your bed." Because then he'd think about sleeping in it—with her. He suppressed a groan.

"Your loss," she said. "I have a feather mattress. And that pullout is one of Mama and Pop's antiques. You know how you can tell a tree's age from the rings in its trunk? You can tell the age of that bed by the number of lumps in its mattress."

"The bed isn't why I can't sleep," he insisted. *She* was.

"Then have some of the punch Pop brought back from the reception." She gestured toward the pitcher on the table. "I can get you a glass with some ice." Drops of condensation ran down the sides of hers, pooling on the tabletop.

"You enjoy your cake. I'll get the ice." He needed something to cool off.

Brenna held her breath until he ducked through the sliding doors into the kitchen. Then she sighed. Coming downstairs for cake had been a mistake. Not because she didn't need the extra calories. She firmly believed what she'd told him— there was *always* room for cake. But because she'd risked running into him. Yet if she were honest with herself, and Brenna was always honest with herself, maybe that was what she'd wanted far more than cake. To see Josh again.

Through the glass doors, she watched him move around the kitchen. He'd discarded the jacket, tie and cummerbund and had undone some of the buttons of his pleated shirt. Dark stubble clung to his jaw, enhancing rather than detracting from his devastating good looks. She closed her eyes against temptation and chided herself. "He's not yours."

"What'd you say?" Josh asked as he stepped out onto the porch again.

Brenna shoved another forkful of moist chocolate cake into her mouth. "Mmm… Good cake."

While his eyes narrowed in apparent suspicion, Josh nodded as if accepting her explanation. He filled his glass from the pitcher and then settled onto the chair across from her. "I wanted to thank you…"

"You already did," she interrupted him.

"I thanked you for your work on the wedding." He laughed. "Or the wedding-that-wasn't."

"You heard that?" What the town gossips had dubbed his cancelled ceremony.

"When they're right…" He sighed. "I appreciate how hard you and your family worked on that, but mostly I wanted to thank you for tonight, for helping me put the boys to bed."

She shrugged. "It was nothing." But it hadn't felt like nothing. It had felt as if *they* were a family. As if *she* were the mom, and those adorable boys were *her* sons, and their handsome father, *her* husband. And that would never be.

He was Molly's man.

"And you couldn't have managed both of them on your own," she pointed out.

He laughed again, his eyes warm with love for his sons. "Oh, I know they're a handful, but I can manage them. I've had to learn."

"You must have help with them."

"Paid help," he admitted. "But for some reason nannies have never seemed to last too long…"

"What about your folks?"

"They're not like yours," he said with an appreciative smile for her parents. "For one thing, they still live in Detroit, where Dad's an automotive engineer. He's always busy with work. And Mom has a heart condition. Weak valves. She doesn't have enough energy to deal with Buzz and TJ."

"I'm sorry about that," Brenna said.

"You're lucky," he said, "that your parents are so…"

"Overwhelming?"

"I was going to say energetic."

She smiled. "They're certainly healthy, so I am lucky. I remember what Molly went through when Mr. McClintock got sick."

"She and I have talked about that."

"She told you?" Despite all their years of friendship, Molly had never talked much with Brenna about losing her father.

"Yeah, it sounds like it was tough on all of them."

"It was toughest on Mrs. McClintock." Brenna sighed. "She lost the love of her life." Was Josh the love of Molly's life? Brenna had always thought that Eric was. But maybe that was just wishful thinking now.

"Molly told me how close her parents were, and how devastated her mother was when her dad died," he said. "My parents have that kind of relationship, too. That strong bond, that love and commitment that carries them through sickness and health."

Brenna was moved by the longing in his voice. "You want that, too?"

His gaze met hers and held. "Doesn't everyone?"

She nodded, then cleared her throat and asked, "Have you heard from Molly?"

"She left me a voice mail." He lifted the glass to his lips, swallowed a mouthful, and then coughed and sputtered. "What's in this?"

"Spikes. Or nails."

"What?"

"That was Buzz and TJ's interpretation of Nick telling them the punch bowl had been spiked."

His eyes rounded. "They didn't have…"

She shook her head. "No. So can you tell me what she said? Or is it too personal? I don't want to pry, but…" She damn well wanted to know what explanation her friend had given for backing out.

He lifted his shoulders in a slight shrug. "She didn't say much. She's sorry. She hopes I understand."

"Do you?"

He rose from his chair and walked toward the railing to stare across the moonlit garden. "She came to see me last night and admitted she was having doubts."

From his tone, Brenna suspected Molly wasn't the only one who'd been having doubts. Or was that more wishful thinking on her part? "If she was having doubts, then she did the right thing by not marrying you. Granted, she could have handled things better, so that you weren't…"

"Humiliated?" Josh asked when her voice trailed off into the darkness. "I wasn't, really. Hell, I should be used to women running out on me." He pushed a hand through his hair, then laughed at himself. "Damn, don't I sound full of self-pity?"

"You're entitled," Brenna said as she stood and joined him at the rail. Stepping close to him, she patted his arm as her dad would have done.

But she didn't have Pop's massive hands or his strength. Her pat was gentle, her touch lingering as the heat of her palm penetrated the thin material of his shirt. His skin tingled, and his body tensed.

"You've had a bad day," she said, almost as if he was one of the twins and she was excusing a temper tantrum.

"No, I think Nick's right," he admitted. "Although I'll deny it if you tell him that."

She laughed. "Okay, your secret's safe with me."

He wondered. Would she keep his real secret—that he was more attracted to her than he'd ever been to the woman he was supposed to have married that day?

"I have bad judgment," he shared. And the fear that he was about to indulge in it again quickened his pulse.

She withdrew her hand from his arm. "Well, I have to argue with you there. Molly is my friend."

"She's my friend, too." But just a friend. He'd have to tell Molly that—if she came back and expected him to go through with the wedding. Even though he hated to break his promise and risk hurting her, he couldn't marry her. "And she's great. Hell, so was Amy. She was just too young. So Nick's only half-right. But it's not the women. It's *my* judgment. It's *me*— I'm the problem."

"I find that hard to believe—unless you have a whole other side of your personality, and I doubt that," she said, narrowing her eyes as if studying him. "So tell me, *are* you Dr. Jekyll and Mr. Hyde?"

He shook his head. "Nope. What you see is what you get." He snorted. "Apparently the women I've been married to—or engaged to—don't want what they see."

"I can't believe that," Brenna said, her voice a sexy rasp. Her eyes glinted in the moonlight and she stared up at him as a bride might her groom on their wedding night.

This was supposed to be *his* wedding night. Brenna Kelly was the maid of honor and not his bride. But he'd never been as attracted to *either* of his brides as he was to her.

He reached for her, pulling her into his arms. His fingertips shaking, he skimmed them along her jaw and lifted her face toward his. "Brenna…"

She lifted her hands between them, as if to push against him and free herself. But instead her palms skimmed over his chest, touching skin left bare by his partially unbuttoned shirt, and her breath audibly caught. Her voice tinged with confusion and longing, she murmured, "Josh…"

Her lips parted on his name and he kissed her, his mouth moving hungrily over hers. She tasted of the chocolate cake with butter-cream frosting her parents had baked for his wedding, but she was far sweeter than any bakery confection. Electrified by the touch of her hands moving over his chest, Josh deepened the kiss, sliding his tongue between her lips.

But then Brenna shoved him back against the railing and pulled herself out of his arms. She stared up at him, her eyes horrified, before running back into the house.

Alone again on the porch, Josh turned to the railing and wrapped his hands tightly around the wood when he would have rather had them wrapped around her.

"Yup." He sighed, his breath a ragged noise on the quiet night air. "I should be used to women running out on me."

A FLOORBOARD CREAKED outside Brenna's door. He'd followed her upstairs? Her heart pounded with fear—not of Josh, but of herself. If he knocked, she'd let him in. She wouldn't be able to help herself. But the footsteps continued past her room to the one next door. The boys. One of them must have gotten up to use the bathroom.

Her breath shuddered out and she flopped back against her pillows. Not that she'd been sleeping. She'd been upstairs only a few minutes, cursing herself for how she'd betrayed Molly. How could she have kissed her best friend's fiancé?

Sick with guilt, she stared up at the canopy that was draped over the four posters of her antique bed. From the canopy to the rosebud-patterned chintz on the curved window seat in the turret, the room belonged to a little girl. Even though she'd lost out on the house she'd fallen in love with, she knew she needed to keep looking. She loved her parents, but she couldn't be their little girl forever. Time to grow up and take the responsibility for her personal life that she'd accepted in her professional life when she'd taken Kelly Confections national.

Time to take responsibility for what she'd done tonight, too. Hand trembling, she fumbled next to the bed for the phone. Unconcerned with the late hour—or early hour— she dialed a number, which went directly to voice mail. "Molly, please call me back. I need to talk to you. I need to know what happened today." She glanced at the clock, the time illuminated in glowing pink. "What happened yesterday."

She sighed. "Most of all, I need to know that you're all right. It's not like you to do this, to back out when you've given your word."

Brenna had suspected for some time that Molly really didn't want to be a doctor. For God's sake, she'd passed out in the delivery room when Abby had given birth to Lara. She'd claimed it was because she hadn't gotten enough sleep, but Brenna had wondered. Yet Molly had continued with med school, refusing to back out on the promise she'd made her father on his deathbed—that she'd become a doctor to save people just as she'd wished she could have saved him.

"Molly, you can talk to me, you know, about anything. We've been friends since preschool. Remember that first day? That bully pulled your pigtail, and I pushed him down and sat on him. When Eric came to Cloverville in second grade you didn't need me to fight your battles anymore. But I still will. Just give me the word if I need to push someone down and sit on them." She laughed. "Because I can hurt them a helluva lot more now."

Her words shuddered out with the hint of a sob. "Most of all, I need to tell you what happened today. I...I...I can't tell you over the phone. Please, Molly, come home." She dropped the cordless back onto the charger and flopped against the pillows again. But she wouldn't sleep. She didn't want to because she already knew what she'd dream about. Josh's kiss.

Josh leaned against the doorjamb, every muscle rigid as he fought the desire to turn around and knock on Brenna's door. It had taken all his willpower to walk past. He shouldn't have even come up here, but he had to check on his boys. Often when they fell asleep as they had— in the coatroom of the American Legion Hall—they woke in the middle of the night, thirsty or hungry, and wide-eyed and ready to play. He didn't want them playing in the Kelly museum of antiques without supervision. Hell, *he* shouldn't have been playing without supervision, either.

He ran his thumb across his lower lip, tasting traces of frosting and Brenna. TJ thrashed about on the full-size bed he shared with Buzz, swinging his arm across his brother's face. Josh grimaced as bone connected with nose cartilage.

"Hey!" Buzz groaned, kicking at his brother.

TJ jabbed with his fists. Buzz head-butted his twin.

They were awake now.

"Hey, settle down," Josh whispered, sitting down on the bed next to Buzz. Springs creaked beneath his weight, the brass frame weak with age. That fragility—and the boys' restlessness—was why he preferred the lumpy foldout bed to sharing this one with his sons. And with him in the parlor, Brenna wasn't quite so temptingly close.

"You two have to go back to sleep," he said, and he wedged his body between them, depressing the mattress so that a twin rolled against each of his sides. He wrapped his arms around the boys, holding them close. And his heart expanded, as it always did, barely able to contain his all-encompassing love for his children.

"I'm not tired," TJ insisted.

"Me, neither," Buzz agreed, his eyes bleary as he blinked his heavy lids. "I can't sleep with *him*. He hogs the bed."

"*You* hog," TJ argued.

"You can sleep in your old beds tomorrow," Josh promised, his neck aching as he crooked it away from the headboard.

"You're gonna unpack 'em here?" TJ asked.

"Yeah," Buzz said, his bottom lip forming his trademark pout, "'cause you packed up all our stuff."

"Even most of our toys," TJ accused with the faint belligerence that usually preceded a temper tantrum.

"We sold our house," Josh reminded them. Although it hadn't been much of a house, with its two small bedrooms and postage-stamp-size yard. But that had been all he could afford while he was working off the student loans for tuition not covered by scholarships.

"And we bought a new house," TJ remembered.

"Shh," Buzz said. "We can't tell Uncle Nick."

"It's not a secret anymore. He knows."

"It's not a secret if you tell it," TJ reprimanded him.

Would Brenna keep their kiss a secret or would she tell Molly? Molly was her best friend—of course she'd tell her. Not that it would make any difference between him and Molly. He didn't intend to marry her now. But he didn't want to cause trouble between Molly and Brenna.

"It's okay."

"So are we moving into the new house tomorrow?" Buzz asked, his fuzzy head rubbing against Josh's shoulder.

"No." He eased a hand over Buzz's hair, then TJ's. "We can't." Not for two weeks. But maybe that would change. Maybe he wouldn't move at all. "We're going to go stay with Uncle Nick for a couple of weeks. All our stuff is at his house."

Nick hadn't even bitched that much about the pyramid of boxes that was piled in the living room of his condo. The boys were supposed to have stayed with him while Josh was on his honeymoon. "And he even set up your beds in his spare room."

"I don't wanna stay with Uncle Nick," TJ whined, his lids beginning to droop like Buzz's. "I wanna stay here. With Mama and Pop and Brenna."

"Me, too," his twin agreed.

Me, too. "We can't stay here," Josh said.

A tear streaked from the corner of Buzz's eye, soaking Josh's shirt. "But we like it here." He sniffed.

"They got a big yard," TJ pointed out.

"And good food."

Josh cooked. When he had time. Or he ordered in. The boys actually preferred when he ordered in.

"Don't make us leave," Buzz whined.

Guilt tightened the muscles in Josh's chest. He hadn't just screwed up his life with another impulsive action. He'd screwed up theirs, too.

Chapter Five

Unable to stall any longer, Brenna descended the stairs, drawn toward the racket in the kitchen. Giggling boys, her father's animated voice, her mother's softer tones…

Where was Josh? He stood on the bottom step of the elaborate mahogany stairwell, as if he'd been waiting for her so long he'd been about to come up and find her. Today he wore jeans and a knit shirt in a blue nearly as deep as his eyes. The outfit had undoubtedly been packed for his honeymoon—the one that he would now spend with Brenna instead of his bride.

Hands trembling slightly, she smoothed them over the cool cotton of her green sundress. She hadn't dressed up for him. She most always wore skirts or dresses since they fit better and were easier to deal with than trying to stuff her fanny into a pair of jeans.

Josh's gaze briefly slid over her before he glanced at his watch and then remarked with a wry grin, "I'm glad you managed to sleep in."

"Kellys are bakers," she reminded him. "We don't ever sleep in."

"Then the boys must be going to become bakers," he

said as he rubbed a hand over his jaw, the shadow darker than the night before. Perhaps he'd forgotten to pack a razor. "They never sleep past seven."

And they hadn't that morning, either, as they'd jumped onto her bed at six-thirty. While her feather mattress didn't have much bounce, that hadn't stopped them from leaping up and down on it—and her.

"Course you know that," he said, "I heard them go into your room."

"You heard them?"

He nodded. "I'm sorry they bothered you," he said of his sons.

"They're no bother," she assured him.

"No, we've already established that *I'm* the bother," he said. His eyes darkened with regret. "I'm so sorry about last night. I lied to you—I guess I *am* Dr. Jekyll and Mr. Hyde. And Dr. Jekyll needs to apologize for Mr. Hyde. You must think I'm such a creep."

"You don't need to be sorry," she interrupted his apology. "You'd had a helluva day. Your ego was bruised, not to mention your heart. You were hurting."

"That's no excuse for taking advantage of you," he said. Obviously he'd been beating himself up over that kiss, and now probably more than his ego was bruised. "You and your parents opened your home to me and my sons. And I repaid your kindness like that?" He shook his head. "Of course we'll find another place to stay, or we'll go back to Grand Rapids."

"That's not necessary, really," she heard herself say when she should have just nodded and let him leave. That would have been the smart thing to do. "I'm actually almost never home."

"Pop mentioned that."

"Yes, the bakery is only open until noon on Sundays, so I don't bother going in. That's why I'm home today. But every other day I leave at daybreak and don't come home until after dark." She'd stretched her hours a bit, but she fully intended to hold herself to that schedule while Josh and the boys were staying with them.

He shook his head. "I don't feel right about this. Things are going to be awkward between us because of what I did."

"Mr. Hyde," she reminded him. "Because of what Mr. Hyde did."

"I wish I could blame someone else."

Blame me. She'd wanted him to kiss her. Staring over his head at the paisley-patterned wallpaper of the hall and foyer, she inhaled a deep breath. "We'll forget last night ever happened."

"Are you sure?" he asked, his gaze intent on her face.

That she could forget their kiss? No. In fact she was pretty damned positive she'd never forget it. Her skin warmed with embarrassment and desire. Why him? Why did she have to be so attracted to him? But that was *her* problem, not his. "I'm sure."

"I was so worried that I'd betrayed your trust."

As she had Molly's?

He continued. "I really want to be your friend."

"We are friends," she assured him. Because he, most of all, could *only* be her friend.

Molly would undoubtedly return soon. Especially since, as everyone suspected, she probably hadn't even left Cloverville. And when Molly was back, how would Brenna explain to her friend that her maid of honor had kissed the groom? She had no excuse for betraying a more than twenty-year-long friendship in that way.

The screen door rattled as someone knocked. Josh peered down the hall toward the foyer and groaned. "Nick." He pushed a hand through his hair. "Now there's a friend I don't need to see right now."

"He's here?"

"He must have kept the directions I gave him for the rehearsal dinner."

"But he didn't show."

"He was working." Josh sighed. "But he should have showed up. He didn't know anyone's names yesterday. Of course, he's always been bad with names." His mouth lifted in a wry grin. "He refers to his patients by their diagnoses and surgical procedures."

But Josh wouldn't do that. Even though she had never seen him at work, Brenna instinctively knew that Josh would have a warm, charming bedside manner. Patients were people to him, and not just ailments.

She reached out to pat his arm, but then pulled her hand back before she touched him, remembering what had happened the last time she had.

"Go in the kitchen," she advised him. Noise drifted from the room in the back of the house, running footsteps, more giggling and then the crash of something breaking.

Josh grimaced. "I'd better, just to relieve your parents. And reimburse them."

"Don't worry about it." She waved off his concern. Her parents wouldn't care, no matter what had broken, but she knew that their house, with all its antiques and collectibles, made people nervous. Her friends had usually preferred the sturdier no-frills McClintock house to the Kellys'. "And don't worry about Nick. I'll take care of the best man."

"Thanks," Josh said. And he touched her then, just skimming his knuckles over her bare shoulder.

But it was enough to have her pulse quickening, her senses humming. She drew in a breath, not exhaling until he left her alone in the hall. She waited another moment before greeting his fair-haired friend at the door. "Good morning, Nick."

Dr. Jameson had obviously stayed in town, maybe even in his car, judging from how bedraggled he looked in his rumpled dress shirt and trousers. If he'd come over to convince Josh to go back to Grand Rapids, maybe she should let him do it. For Nick's peace of mind *and* hers.

"Hi…" His green eyes skimmed her face as if he were searching for a name.

"Brenna," she reminded him. "My name is Brenna."

"Brenna Kelly. Yeah, I know."

She arched an eyebrow, skeptical of his claim. But she didn't care if he remembered her name. She just wanted him to take care of his friend so she wouldn't try to, as she usually tried to take care of everyone else. Another Kelly habit. One she intended to break now, along with her promise to get rid of Nick, as she offered, "I'll get Josh for you."

"No!"

The urgency in Nick Jameson's voice stopped her, and she turned back.

"I'd like to talk to you." He swallowed hard. "Brenna."

She pushed open the screen door by its purple-painted frame and stepped out to join him on the porch. Cold, despite the warm morning air, Brenna crossed her arms over her chest and waited for him to say more. Despite walking down the aisle together yesterday, they'd barely spoken to each other. She didn't know Nick Jameson at all. She didn't know why Josh had chosen him as his best man, especially since he hadn't even wanted to face the man this morning.

His voice gruff with impatience, Nick said, "You need to tell your friend to come home."

"What?"

"You know where the runaway bride is," he accused her.

Brenna didn't know for certain, but if she were a betting woman, she'd bet on Eric South's cabin. She had no intention of sharing that information with Nick Jameson, however. She'd already betrayed Molly. Brenna reminded him of the note the bride had left. "She asked for some time alone."

"Don't you think that's pretty damned selfish of her?" Nick asked, his eyes ablaze with indignation.

"You obviously don't know Molly," she observed. If he were really Josh's best friend, how could he *not* know Molly? "She is probably the least selfish person I know."

"I *don't* know her," he admitted. "She was supposed to marry my best friend, and I barely know her name."

"Well, you're bad with names."

He laughed. "Josh has been talking to you."

She nodded.

"That's good," he said, exhaling loudly with obvious relief.

She studied him through narrowed eyes. "You're worried about him."

"Yes, I am," he admitted. "He's determined to talk to her and work things out."

Her stomach clenched as it had when the boys—jumping on her bed—had inadvertently stepped on it, digging their bare toes into her belly. No, this hurt worse, knowing how

Josh felt. She didn't doubt that Nick knew. Even though she didn't understand why, the two men were close.

The blond doctor persisted, "So you need to tell your friend to come home."

"Molly. Her name is Molly." The woman Josh loved. He hadn't meant to kiss *her*, and Brenna knew that. He'd been distraught over being jilted.

"I know her name," Nick insisted. "I wish Josh would forget it. I wish he'd forget all about her."

Brenna was startled by his declaration. "Then I don't understand why you want her to come home."

"He can't forget her until he talks to her."

Despite the ache that was still gnawing at her, Brenna smiled. "You really don't know Molly. Men don't forget Molly." Every male from grade school through grad school, had fallen for Molly's big, dark eyes and gentle spirit. "Seeing her again isn't going to get him to change his mind about moving here or about opening the office that I know you were against opening here. Bringing Molly back won't get you what you want."

Nor Brenna. Because, God help her, she wanted Josh.

"This isn't about what I want." Nick pushed his hand through his hair. "No, it is, because I want my friend to be happy. If moving to Cloverville makes him happy, I'll go along with it. I just want Josh to be *happy.*"

That was all a good friend should want for the people he cared about, their happiness even more than his own. She smiled, genuinely, at him and acknowledged, "Now I understand."

"What?"

"Why you're his best friend," she explained. "Now I understand."

Nick nodded. His voice deep with pride, he said, "I *am* his best friend."

Images, some more than twenty years old, flitted through her mind. Of her and Molly, friends since childhood, sharing everything from cupcakes to makeup. Molly standing beside her mom at her father's funeral, holding her up, holding her family together every bit as much as Clayton had. Molly was the strongest person Brenna knew. Her voice breaking with emotion, she told Nick, "I'm Molly's best friend, you know."

She blinked back tears and a surge of guilt over what she'd done. She wouldn't betray her friend again. Not for *anyone*. "She wants time alone, and she's getting time alone. I'm not telling you where she is."

"I understand that you're protecting your friend," he said with a respectful bob of his head. "I just want to protect mine."

"Protect Josh? From what?" Did Nick Jameson realize that Brenna had feelings for his friend that she had no business feeling?

Josh pushed open the screen door and answered her question. "Nick thinks I need protecting from myself."

Damn. He should have known better than to leave Nick alone with Brenna. Who knew what Nick had told her? He could only imagine, and regrettably he was good at imagining. He'd spent the entire night envisioning what could have happened between the two of them, if she hadn't run away from him.

And he'd concluded that Nick was right—he should go back to Grand Rapids. Because he was doing it again, falling too fast, rushing into another relationship. This time even before his last one officially had ended. When was he ever going to learn from his mistakes? No wonder Nick worried about him.

His friend's eyes narrowed as he intently studied Josh. "You okay?"

Josh nodded, but he doubted Nick would fall for a lie. He wasn't okay, not with his mind full of thoughts of Brenna—who leaned against the porch railing watching them. The early morning breeze ruffled her waves of red hair. Josh pulled his gaze away from her and focused on his friend. "Fine. I'm fine."

Nick sniffed the air. "Cinnamon rolls," he murmured.

"Fresh from the oven," Pop said as he flung open the screen door. "Get in here before the boys eat 'em all."

Josh suppressed a groan. He appreciated Mr. Kelly's generosity, but he knew sugar and his sons was not a good combination.

"You, too," Pop said, pointing at Nick. "You're the best man."

And just because Nick was Josh's friend, he was welcome? Josh shook his head at this family's generosity. He didn't want to take advantage of it, the way he'd nearly taken advantage of Brenna last night.

Nick had no such qualms. "You don't happen to have an extra room, do you?" he asked. "Since I have the next couple of weeks off, I thought I'd stay in town."

Because he hadn't been able to talk Josh into leaving. "There's no reason for you to stay," Josh assured his overprotective friend.

"Of course there is," Nick continued as he followed Brenna and her dad down the hall toward the kitchen. "I can keep an eye on the construction for the office building."

The construction was nearly done—Nick wouldn't like

that. He hadn't agreed with Josh about picking Cloverville as the location of the private practice they'd first planned in their teens. He'd wanted to stay closer to the hospital where they'd still have surgical privileges, and where Nick intended to stay on staff. Josh wanted to do more than surgery. He wanted to take care of people—most of all his sons.

They sat on stools at the huge kitchen island, their faces covered in icing and the cinnamon rolls clutched tightly in their hands. As he smiled at them, he caught Nick's shoulder with his hand and squeezed out a warning. "There's no room here." Then he pitched his voice lower, and added, "And no reason for you to stay."

"Then let's go back to Grand Rapids," Nick said.

Josh shook his head. "There's no reason for *you* to stay." But he had one. Actually he had two reasons, his boys. They loved Cloverville. And the Kellys.

"So there's really no room for me stay?" Nick asked Brenna as she walked him to the door.

She smiled at his persistence. "I'm sorry. No." Her parents would have found room, though, if not for the subtle shake of Josh's head when they'd opened their mouths to offer. He obviously didn't want his friend staying with them. "There aren't any hotels or motels in Cloverville, either. I'm really sorry."

But she wasn't. To protect her friend she couldn't have Nick around looking for Molly, stealing from her that time she'd asked for—that time she'd never taken for herself. Everything she'd focused on since her dad had died had been connected to getting the medical degree she'd promised him.

Poor Molly. She deserved some happiness in her life; she deserved a man like Josh.

"Clayton McClintock offered me his spare room," Nick admitted. "I think *he* feels guilty about the way his sister's treated Josh."

"Molly has a good reason for doing what she did." She had to, or maybe she'd cracked under the pressure she'd put on herself. Last night at the reception Brenna had been ready to disregard her friend's request for time alone, and Eric had been right to point out her selfishness. She shouldn't have called and left the late-night voice mail, either, because that had been to relieve her own guilt. A good friend gave a person what she wanted—including time.

"Josh is fine," she assured Nick, pitching her voice low so that he wouldn't overhear them from the powder room off the hall, where he was cleaning up the twins. The hall which had once been wide, was narrow with the antique desks and wall tables that lined it.

Brenna wanted a house that was wide open for herself. And she wanted nothing breakable in her home, in her life—especially not her heart. She couldn't let herself fall for Josh or his sons. She didn't have that right.

"I'd like to believe Josh is fine," Nick said, "but I've made that mistake before."

About Josh? "I don't understand…"

The tall man stepped closer. "Just keep an eye on him for me. And if he starts acting crazy, call me." He pressed a card into her hand. "My cell number's on there."

"What do you mean, crazy?" Like kissing her in the moonlight? *That* had been crazy.

"Just, you know, depressed or…"

"Good, you're still here," Josh said as he stepped through the pocket doors of the powder room and joined them. With his jaw clenched and his eyes narrowed, he hardly looked happy.

Brenna curled her hand around Nick's card, as if to hide it from Josh. Somehow, she doubted he'd be pleased his friend was so worried about him. His pride had already taken enough of a beating.

With a hand on each of his son's shoulders, Josh nudged them forward. "Have fun with Uncle Nick," he told them.

"What?" Nick asked, his eyes widening in surprise. "You're not going on your honeymoon, so why would I take Buzz and TJ?"

"You're taking them to the park," Josh said, a wicked grin illuminating his face.

"We wanna go to the park, Uncle Nick," TJ said, reaching for the surgeon's hand.

"Yeah, the park," Buzz chimed in.

"They have to burn off some of that sugar," Josh explained, as he held open the screen door that led to the front porch.

Nick groaned, and then nodded. "Sure, we'll go to the park." He tightened his grip around each boy's hand as he stepped outside. "We have to stop someplace first, though, and it's probably a good idea to have you both along."

Brenna wondered at Dr. Jameson's cryptic comment. But then the boys jerked free of his grasp and turned back to her. "Bye, Brenna," they shouted.

Her heart warmed. "See you both later." She wasn't so sure about Nick, and wondered if he would survive the adventure at the park. She leaned over and pressed a kiss to each twin's cheek.

"Remember to call," Nick beseeched her.

She nodded, then joined Josh on the porch, where he

waved to his sons and his friend. "He was really going to watch them while you were on your honeymoon?" she asked, amazed that the other doctor would have agreed. "How did you convince him?"

Josh's broad shoulders lifted in a shrug. "Even though he won't admit it, he actually enjoys spending time with them. When Amy left me, he helped a lot with them. Too bad he's sworn off marriage and kids."

"Too bad," she agreed, remembering the way Colleen had stared up at Nick when she'd danced with him the night before. Brenna would have to warn her young friend to protect her heart, as well.

"Yeah, too bad." Josh sighed. "He'd make a good husband and father."

"He's some loyal friend," Brenna mused. Usually the people who made friends like that *were* friends like that themselves, loyal and supportive.

"Yeah, Nick and I go way back."

Just as she and Molly did. She should be unconditionally supportive of Molly, as Nick was of Josh. Yet while she was concerned about Molly, she was also confused. How could her friend have been so careless with Josh's feelings, with his heart? "You two have a 'from the cradle to the grave' kind of friendship?"

"That's what Nick's afraid of," Josh said. "That he's going to be putting me in the grave."

"What?"

"I heard him, asking you to keep an eye on me for him, when he realized there wasn't room for him to stay here." Josh snorted. "Hell, I'm surprised he didn't bring in a sleeping bag so he could sack out on the floor next to me in the parlor."

"Well, that goes beyond friendship and qualifies as obsession," she observed, leaning over the rail to catch a glimpse of Nick with the boys as they disappeared down the sidewalk. "Are you sure you should let him take your sons?"

Josh nodded. "He's fine with Buzz and TJ. I'm the one he's driving crazy."

"Why's he so worried about you?" she asked, wondering if she needed to be worried, too.

"He's got me on suicide watch."

Brenna's heart skipped a beat. "Suicide watch?"

"Yeah." Josh nodded. "He's worried I'm going to do something stupid."

"So he said," she admitted. "But he wouldn't tell me what he considered stupid."

"He thinks he has reason to be worried," Josh admitted.

"Oh, my God!" Realization dawned. "When your wife left you, did you do something?"

"No!" Josh assured her. "I never even considered it, not even for a second. My sons depend solely on me."

"I can't imagine what kind of woman would leave her children."

"Marriage, motherhood… She was overwhelmed."

"You must have been, too," she pointed out.

"Things were crazy for a while," Josh admitted, rubbing a hand across the stubble on his chin. His razor had disappeared from his overnight bag, and he hoped Buzz hadn't gotten a hold of it again. The kid would need more stitches, if he cut his hair any shorter. "But I never got crazy."

She held up the card he'd seen Nick press into her hand. "I don't need this?"

He shook his head. "No. Nick's overly sensitive."

She rolled her eyes.

"He's overly sensitive about this." He grimaced, re-membering and reliving his friend's pain. "When his older brother's wife left him, the guy fell apart. Nick and I were just teenagers at the time. He didn't know how to help his brother, and then it was too late."

"He killed himself?"

Josh pushed his hand through his hair. "Let's say it was a deliberate accident."

Her green eyes widened. "Oh, my God. That's awful…"

Josh appreciated her reaction. Then he noticed the way she stared at him, as if wondering whether he might do the same.

"I'm fine," he assured her, although he was getting sick of having to make the claim. He thought about proving it to her, that he hadn't loved her friend and that he wasn't bro-kenhearted. He reached out, as he had last night, sliding his fingers across the silky skin of her cheek. He'd eaten more than one cinnamon roll, but still he was hungry—for her.

Her breath audibly caught. "Josh…"

She'd run from him last night, like every other woman he'd cared about or thought he might have cared about. It was better that she thought he was in love with Molly then maybe he wouldn't fall in love with her. He pulled his hand away from her face and lifted his fingers to his lips as if licking away frosting. "The boys iced you, like the cinnamon rolls."

Brenna nodded, but Josh doubted she bought his claim about the icing—or about being fine.

Chapter Six

"He's fine," Brenna assured herself as she helped her mother carry brunch to the table. No matter that they'd had cinnamon rolls earlier that morning, Sunday brunch was mandatory. No one missed a meal at the Kelly house.

"He is," Mama agreed, pausing to press her cheek against her daughter's head as she set out sausage gravy to go with the flaky buttermilk rolls that Brenna had just pulled from the oven. "I don't understand what Molly was thinking," the older woman said as she stared out the sliding doors. Like Brenna, her attention was focused on the backyard, where Josh wrestled with his boys.

Brenna nodded, equally puzzled.

"Mary McClintock called earlier today," Mama said as she backed away from the table toward the island in the middle of the industrial-sized kitchen. While they'd kept the rest of the house true to the Victorian era, they'd modernized the kitchen, installing commercial-quality stainless-steel appliances, granite countertops and cherry cabinets.

"Did she talk to Molly?" Brenna asked. If she were Molly, she would have called her mother—right after she called her best friend. But despite having known her longer and being college roommates, Molly wasn't as close to Brenna as she was to Eric South. Probably especially now—physically, at least.

"She didn't say," her mother replied, her gaze not quite meeting Brenna's. "She called to check on her almost-son-in-law and the boys. She wanted to make sure everything was all right over here."

"She offered to put them up at her house, didn't she?" Brenna deduced from her mother's evasiveness.

Mama waved a hand, dismissing the idea. "That would be silly. They'd be stacked on top of each other over there, with Abby and Lara staying, along with Mary's own kids."

Just fourteen-year-old Rory and twenty-three-year-old Colleen. Clayton had his own place in town above his father's old insurance agency, which was his now.

"Abby's staying in Cloverville?" Brenna asked after the friend who'd spent the past eight years between Detroit and Chicago. Like Brenna, Abby loved business. She'd started her own firm from the ground up—Temps To Go, a specialized employment agency. "She and Lara are moving home? Cloverville would be a great place for the next branch of Abby's business."

Mama held up a hand to restrain Brenna's enthusiasm. "Abby claims she's just staying until she's sure Molly's okay. But if Mary has her way, Abby and that adorable daughter of hers will be home for good."

Brenna narrowed her eyes at her mother's odd tone. Was she planning to play matchmaker, as Mary McClintock always had? Of course, Mrs. McClintock had tried matching up Eric with Molly and that had never worked out. Molly had always insisted they were just friends, that Eric didn't have any romantic feelings for her. Yet she'd been devastated when he'd enlisted in the Marines. Their friendship or whatever it was that existed between the two of them had never been the same after that.

Maybe Mrs. McClintock would have more luck connecting Abby and Clayton. Brenna smiled as she remembered their kiss on the dance floor. Apparently the two of them couldn't fight their attraction quite as successfully as they had eight years before.

"I'll have to call Abby," Brenna said, "and see if I can help convince her to stay."

"Mary said that the best man stopped by her house this morning with Buzz and TJ."

"He did?" Was that the visit he'd curiously referred to?

"Yes, to see Colleen."

So Nick hadn't just accidentally run into her at the park, as he'd led them to believe when he'd brought the boys home. Nick had been invited to brunch when he'd arrived, but he'd begged off, probably exhausted from the outing. From the boys or from trying to pry Molly's whereabouts out of Colleen? Brenna suppressed a smile. No one could keep a secret like the youngest McClintock sister.

"Does Mrs. McClintock know if Colleen talked to her sister?"

"You're worried about her," Mama guessed. "You and Molly have always been so close."

"Yes." Brenna sighed. "That's why I just can't understand…"

Mama shook her head, tumbling the waves of white hair around her face. "I don't understand Molly agreeing to be Josh's bride…" she said with another shake of her head "…when we all know she's always loved Eric South."

Brenna laughed. "You have that backward. Eric has

always loved *her.*" Since second grade when he'd moved to Cloverville to live with his great uncle. While the McClintocks had been through a rough time, no one member of their group of friends had experienced as much loss as Eric. First, both his parents had died, and then the guardians with whom his parents had left him had gotten divorced. And neither of them had wanted him. Fortunately his uncle Harold, a retired Marine colonel, had been delighted to have him.

"Eric South has grown into a fine man," Mama said with pride. She and Mary McClintock had been like mothers to him. "He's a hero, you know."

"I know." Even before he'd gotten hurt in the line of duty, saving others, he'd been a hero. Molly's hero. Brenna sighed. "But Molly has only ever seen him as a friend."

Which was the only way Brenna could allow herself to see Josh. But as he and his boys joined her family at the table, she couldn't help imagining that he was hers.

"YOU'RE BACK," Josh said with a sigh as his friend walked up the wide steps of the Kellys' front porch for the third time that day. Obviously his best friend had gone home to Grand Rapids for a bit, since he'd replaced his rumpled tux with a fresh pair of jeans. A picnic basket swung from his free hand. "You brought me food? Did you forget where I'm staying?"

Josh had just pushed himself away from the brunch table. In addition to a second batch of cinnamon rolls, there'd been frittata, sausage gravy and homemade biscuits, eggs and bacon. He'd never eaten so well, and neither had Buzz and TJ. He doubted they'd settle for his boxed macaroni and cheese and cold sandwiches ever again. Maybe Mama Kelly—or Brenna—could teach him how to cook.

Nick glanced down at the picnic basket, and his face flooded with color. "Uh, this isn't for you. But I did bring you this." He dropped an electric razor into Josh's hand. "You look like hell."

And Nick obviously didn't want Josh looking like his brother had after his wife had left him. Rubbing a hand over the stubble on his jaw, Josh explained, "My razor disappeared."

Nick nodded. "I figured as much. Like I told Colleen, I really do owe her sister a thank-you."

"For what?"

"If she'd actually married you, you two would be off on your honeymoon right now."

The thought of a honeymoon with Molly filled Josh with dread rather than excitement. He preferred to be right where he was…with Brenna. God, Nick was right. He was crazy.

But he wasn't the only one filled with dread at the thought of his honeymoon. Nick shuddered, as well. "And the twins would be with me."

Josh jabbed his shoulder lightly. "Hey, those are your godsons."

"Yeah, I know." Nick sighed. "And I just paid off the plumbing bill from the last time they stayed with me."

Josh laughed. "C'mon."

"And the cat has just finally ventured out of the closet."

"That cat is skittish."

"Gee, I wonder why."

Josh patted his friend's shoulder again. Changing the subject—back to the one Nick obviously wanted to avoid—he asked, "So if the food isn't for me, who is it for?"

"I'm staying in Cloverville," Nick replied, ignoring Josh's question.

"What? You camping out in the park?" He probably wouldn't get much sleep if so, as Buzz and TJ really liked the playground. They'd already talked Pop and Mama into bringing them back.

Nick shook his head. "No, Clayton's letting me stay in his spare room."

Josh groaned. "C'mon, you can't take advantage of the guy. He's probably not exactly thrilled with us, for not leasing the empty space in his building."

"He understood we needed more room."

And Nick had needed more time—so he'd agreed to open an office in Cloverville only if they built a new building. "You already hate this town," Josh reminded him. "Just go home. I'm fine."

"Have you heard from her?"

"Molly?"

"Yeah, you know, the woman who was supposed to marry you yesterday."

"No." He'd decided to not tell Nick about her voice mail—he'd only be more pissed off if he heard about her cryptic message.

"Then I'm staying in Cloverville until I find her for you," Nick insisted.

Josh sighed. "You don't need to do that."

"I'm the best man," Nick said, with a teasing glint in his eyes, as if he spoke of more than merely his role in the wedding party. "It's one of my duties to track down the runaway bride."

Josh grimaced. "Funny, I don't remember that being on Brenna's list."

"Of course not." Nick laughed. "She's protecting her friend."

"You think she knows where Molly is?"

Nick nodded. "I'm sure of it. All those bridesmaids know. Clayton's gonna work on Abby."

"And who are you working on?"

His friend glanced at his watch. "Gotta go," he said as he headed back down the stairs to the sidewalk.

"Nick!" Josh yelled after his best friend, but the guy simply kept walking, whistling under his breath.

Josh grinned. Well, if Nick had planned a picnic in the park, he wasn't going to get the privacy he no doubt wanted. He turned back to the house. But the grin slid from his face as he remembered that when Pop and Mama had taken the boys, they'd left him alone with Brenna.

"I CAN'T BELIEVE the boys wanted to go back to the park," Brenna mused as she submerged the quiche plate in a sinkful of soapy water. And she couldn't believe that her parents had taken them, leaving her and Josh to clean up the mess from brunch alone.

Were *her* parents matchmaking now? She was used to their pressure for grandchildren, but she hadn't thought they'd stoop to underhanded tactics such as taking advantage of a man who was brokenhearted and vulnerable. She couldn't believe *she* nearly had the night before.

"There's a playground there," Josh said, as if that explained his sons' motives.

What about her parents'?

Josh stood beside her at the sink, drying dishes with the same precision he probably demonstrated in his surgeries. His shoulder brushed against her bare one as he reached above her to put away a plate.

"But Nick said Buzz nearly got sick from the merry-go-round," Brenna said. The kid had come home a little green that morning—and so had Nick.

"That'll just make them want to ride it more," their father said with a chuckle. "They don't learn from their mistakes." The amusement left his face. "I guess they get that from me."

"Don't be so hard on yourself," she advised. Perhaps Nick was right about his friend, that he needed someone to keep an eye on him. She wished that was the reason she'd insisted that he and his boys stay with her family, but she couldn't be sure her reasons hadn't been more selfish than altruistic… Because she would miss him…

"I try to do the right thing for my boys—" Josh said as he dropped the dish towel onto the counter "—but all I seem to do is make things worse."

"Staying here is going to make things worse?" she wondered.

He nodded. "They're going to get too attached to your parents. And to you."

"I see. That's why you were going to go back to Grand Rapids." She'd worried that maybe it was because of her.

He jerked his chin in another short nod. "Yes. And I shouldn't have let you change my mind."

"Did you change your mind about moving here?" she asked. It would be easier for them both if he had. If he moved back to Grand Rapids and never set foot in Cloverville again.

"No," he said, "despite Nick's efforts."

Instead of having her hopes dashed, relief eased the pressure on Brenna's chest. She wanted him to stay. "Then it's not a problem that they're becoming attached. They can still come over here, and my folks can visit them at your new house. They can still have a relationship."

"What about us?" he asked.

"What about us?" she repeated as she wrestled again with her unspoken desires.

"Can *we* have a relationship?"

"We're already friends," she reminded him, her heart beating heavily at the intensity of his stare.

"I know." He sighed. "That's all we can be, but I can't help…"

"What, Josh?" She lifted her hands from the sink and wiped them on the towel Josh had left on the granite counter. "What can't you help?"

"Wanting more."

There was no moonlight, no spiked punch. He had to be able to see that she was no substitute for Molly. She wasn't her *second*. Brenna drew in a deep breath and tried to calm her racing pulse. Josh's freshly shaved jaw tempted her to reach out and glide her fingers over the smoothness of his cheek.

"It's okay," she said. "I understand."

"You do?" he asked, as if he didn't.

"You're hurting. Your heart, your pride, over the way Molly jilted you."

Josh winced, not with pain but guilt from letting her think he felt anything but relief over the canceled wedding.

Before he could explain, though, Brenna continued. "I understand that you want to feel better."

"But that's just it," he said, as he reached over and wrapped his arms around her. "I don't know if you'll make me feel better…or worse."

Her breasts were soft against his chest, and her hair brushed his cheek. He wanted her too much to care about the consequences at the moment.

He lowered his head and kissed her—with none of the tentativeness or gentleness of the previous evening. He kissed her with all the passion and frustration he'd suppressed ever since he'd met her.

She pulled back, her lips swollen from the kiss. and protested, "We can't!"

Shaking with desire, he forced himself to drop his arms and step away from her. But then she reached for him, pushing her fingers through his hair to pull his head back down to hers. She kissed him with all the Kelly warmth and generosity, filling his senses and testing his restraint.

He failed. His control snapping, he closed his hands over her hips and lifted her onto the kitchen island. "Brenna…"

"Shh," she murmured against his mouth. Her hands cupped his face, smoothing his jaw. "You're so damned good-looking…"

He'd been complimented before—just the previous evening, in fact, by the town busybodies—but no compliment had ever meant as much to him or had ever felt as sincere. Maybe it was just because his ego had been bruised, but he suspected it had far more to do with who was giving the compliment.

"And you're so beautiful," he replied, awed by her voluptuous beauty and her passion.

Brenna shook her head, as if trying to awaken from a dream. "This isn't real. This can't be happening."

He shook his head. "This… You are the only thing that feels *real* to me. You, Brenna Kelly, you're more *real* than anyone I've ever known."

Brenna had been called *real* before, by her friends and by associates, but never by a man. And never had it meant so much to her. She was down-to-earth and free of pretense.

And open and sometimes too honest, for some people. Josh calling her "real"—that compliment meant more to her than any declaration of beauty. If only another man had said it to her.

If only this man didn't already belong to someone else—to her friend.

She shifted against the counter, but Josh blocked her attempt to get down by standing right in front of her, between her legs. Hip to hip, chest to chest. Why was she—who'd always been so strong—too weak to resist? "Josh…"

"Brenna, let me see how real you are." His hands closed over the straps of her sundress, slipping them from her shoulders. The bodice slid down, revealing a strapless underwire bra in the same emerald green as her dress and her eyes. Maybe she had dressed for him.

So that she would see this look on his face—admiration. And desire.

Then he reached for the clasp at her back, unhooking the bra so that it fell onto her lap. His breath shuddered out. "Brenna…"

Trembling with need, she caught his hands in hers. "*Feel* how real I am," she offered, not even remembering the last time a man had touched her. Knowing no man like this one—so handsome, so gentle—had *ever* touched her before.

When his palms brushed her skin she trembled, wanting and needing more. He gave her more—leaning forward first to kiss her mouth, his tongue flirting with her lips before exploring more deeply. Then his mouth skimmed her jaw and throat, traveling down to the curve of her breasts. She shivered, her nerves never more alive than they were now from his touch.

"What's this?" he asked, his breath warm against her

skin. His fingertip skimmed the side of her breast. "You have a tattoo?"

She nodded. Shivering with cold now, she crossed her arms over her chest. How could she do this? She, who had always been so loyal to her friends?

"About nine years ago, we all got tattoos," she explained. "Well, everyone but Abby, and it had been her idea. I think she came up with it for Molly and Colleen, to distract them because their dad was so sick then. We all piled into her car and drove to Grand Rapids. But thanks to Rory ratting us out, Clayton caught up with us before Abby got hers."

Remembering that day, thinking how happy Molly and Colleen had been after so much stress and sadness, filled her with guilt and regret. "You've never seen Molly's tattoo?"

"Molly and I never…"

She lifted her gaze to his face, hope pounding in her chest again. "You never made love?"

"We were going to wait until…"

"Your honeymoon?" No wonder he'd rushed the wedding. Sweet, old-fashioned Molly. "But you never even…"

"Made out?" He shook his head. "Our relationship wasn't about this." He gestured toward her, his eyes hot with desire.

"What's *this?*" She wanted to know, needing an explanation.

"Passion."

"Lust." Wishing that was all she felt for him.

"It's not like that. It's more. There's more here between us…" He shook his head. "Maybe I am crazy."

"You're not the only one. This isn't me. I can't, but I can't *not*…"

"Can I see your tattoo?" he asked, his eyes wide with curiosity and hope, just like one of his sons using little-boy cuteness to con another cookie from Mama. Or her. God help her, she wanted to give him all her cookies.

Biting her lip, she lowered her arms so he could see the small tattoo on the outer side of one breast.

"It's a cupcake?"

"I have always loved sweets."

He dipped his head, and the tip of his tongue traced the pink-frosted cupcake. "Sweet," he murmured.

"Josh…"

His lips slid over the slope of her breast right to the nipple, which he drew into his mouth.

She bit her lip to hold back a moan and reached up, her hands catching onto the pot rack that was over their heads. She clutched the metal and held tight as his mouth moved to the other breast. His fingers stroked the wet nipple of the abandoned one. It wasn't enough, and she wanted more. She lifted her legs and wound them around his waist, pulling his hips tight against hers. His erection strained his jeans. She shifted into him and he groaned.

He obviously wanted more, too.

"Josh…"

He lifted his head, his gaze hot and hungry for her. "What do you want, Brenna?"

Before she could answer him, the screen door slammed shut and someone stepped into the foyer. A soft, feminine McClintock voice called out, "Hello?"

"Oh, God, it's Molly," Brenna gasped. Scrambling from the counter, she jerked the pot rack she'd been holding onto. Pots and pans rattled, and one fell…on Josh.

On her way to the stairs she glanced back, taking in Josh's stunned expression. From the pan or from the shock of what they had very nearly done?

Chapter Seven

Josh pressed his palms flat against the granite counter, willing his breathing to settle and his heart to stop pounding.

"You okay?" Colleen McClintock, his fiancée's younger sister, asked tentatively as she joined him in the kitchen.

Hell, no. Not after what had just happened—or had just about happened. While his body hummed with frustrated sexual energy, he also breathed a sigh of relief. He wasn't even officially unengaged yet. He had no right to kiss Brenna as he'd kissed her. And certainly no right to want more. "Yeah, sure…"

Colleen stepped forward and kicked one of the pans that had fallen to the floor when Brenna had rattled the rack, which still swayed on the chains suspending it from the ceiling.

"It must have fallen," he murmured.

When Colleen turned away to put it in the sink, Josh surreptitiously rubbed the lump on the back of his head where the frying pan had made contact. *Out of the frying pan, into the fire.* He suppressed a nervous chuckle over the irreverent thought.

"Where is everyone?" Colleen asked as she turned around to face him.

"Mr. and Mrs. Kelly took the boys into town." To the park. But he'd heard something about a promise of ice cream, too. They'd probably be gone a while yet, leaving him alone even longer with their daughter. He should be glad Colleen had arrived when she had.

"And Brenna. Where is she?" her friend asked.

"Uh, Brenna had to…" He noticed her emerald-green bra on the floor at his feet. It was too big for him to hide beneath his shoe, and Colleen might notice his kicking it aside. So he willed her not to look down. "Brenna went upstairs, I think," he stammered. Because she'd thought the intruder was Molly. Guilt flashed through him over the horrible spot in which he'd put them both.

Colleen narrowed her eyes and studied him thoughtfully. "Is everything okay here?"

Josh's gaze slid away from hers, to the bra lying on the hardwood floor. Heat rose to his face. He felt as he had as a teenager when his parents had caught him and his girlfriend necking on the couch in the basement rec room, embarrassed but also ready to explode with frustration. "Uh…"

"Because if it's not, you and the boys can stay with us," she offered. "Rory can sleep in the family room. It's really not a problem. If not for the superstition, my mother would have had you stay with us anyway."

"Maybe she was right to be superstitious," he admitted. But even if they hadn't broken tradition, he doubted the wedding would have happened.

"So, you saw Molly before the wedding."

Thinking of her maid of honor and not Molly, his face flushed. He'd put Brenna in an impossible position. He had to tell her that he hadn't proposed to Molly out of love. That he'd…what? Proposed out of friendship, selfishness? Hell, maybe it was better if she thought love had motivated his proposal. "Uh…"

"I'm sorry. I don't mean to pry," Colleen said, her voice even softer with the apology.

She'd been volunteering at the hospital for years, in the pediatric cancer ward. She was a sweet girl, and while she was shy with adults she was wonderfully animated with children. He had an uneasy feeling that she was the bridesmaid Nick intended to work on with that picnic lunch.

"She's your sister. You're not prying. Really," he insisted, not wanting her to feel badly about asking questions, when she had every right to do so.

Her face flushed pink. "She is my sister. I thought I knew her pretty well. It isn't like Molly to take off the way she did, without any warning."

"She didn't," Josh assured her, recognizing the worship of her older sister. Nick had felt the same way about his big brother, and so Josh understood even though he had no siblings of his own. "I mean, I had some warning."

"You knew she might change her mind?"

Footsteps sounded overhead and a door closed. Brenna had fled the kitchen, fled him and rushed upstairs the minute Colleen had called out. Did she know now that it was not Molly, but Colleen, who sounded similar to her older sister?

He lifted his chin. Staring at the ceiling, he admitted, "I knew."

"Then why…"

Hadn't he cancelled the wedding? He shrugged. They

should have, the night before the ceremony. Molly had admitted to having doubts, to being scared, and he'd known after meeting Brenna that he never would have fallen in love with Molly.

"You don't want to talk about it," she guessed. "I understand."

"That makes one person."

"What? Is someone pressuring you?" She nodded as she answered her own question. "Oh. Nick."

"Yes. Nick." Josh pushed a hand through his hair. The bump had gone down some, but fortunately the hit had been hard enough to knock some sense into his head. "He doesn't understand."

"I'm sorry. I know he's your best friend, but…"

"He means well," Josh defended him. "He may not understand me, but I think I understand him. We go back a long way. He loves me like a brother." Josh sighed. "That's why he's pressuring me to leave Cloverville. He's worried that I might do something crazy."

And like always, Nick had been damn smart to worry. Damn, Josh hated when his friend was right.

"I thought he considered staying in Cloverville crazy."

"Oh, God," Josh said with a groan. "I'm not the only one he's pressuring. I saw the two of you on the dance floor last night. I should have known what he was up to."

"That he only asked me to dance to find out where my sister is?"

"I didn't mean *that*." He shook his head, disgusted with his tactlessness.

Colleen was a sweet girl, a *beautiful* girl. Nick had every reason to be interested in her, but knowing Nick, he probably had only one thing in mind—finding her sister.

His best friend was under the mistaken assumption that Josh would leave Cloverville if he talked to Molly. And even though Josh probably should, he couldn't break his promise to the boys.

"That didn't sound right," he corrected himself. "But you have to know Nick. He's really single-minded."

"I know."

"No, Colleen, you don't know him. No matter how many years you've been volunteering at the hospital, you don't know Nick," Josh said, not wanting the young woman to get hurt. "He lets very few people get close to him."

"You."

"Like I said, we go back a long way. I knew him before…" Before his brother had died, before Nick had shut himself off. "I knew him before he got like this."

"Like *this?*"

"Determined to go it alone, to never get involved with anyone." Josh had thought Nick crazy, but now he realized *he* was the crazy one, desperately trying to find a lasting relationship, like his folks and Brenna's parents had.

"I know," Colleen assured him. "I have been volunteering at the hospital for a few years now. I've heard all the gossip about Dr. Jameson."

Josh nodded. "The sad part is that all the rumors are true. He may date, but he's never really had a serious relationship."

"I understand not wanting to fall in love. The risk is too great."

Josh laughed. Even this young girl understood that. Why had he been so slow?

"Is she gone?" Brenna asked as she joined Josh in the kitchen. She'd exchanged her sundress for a lightweight sweater and a long denim skirt. The weather had grown cooler as dark clouds rolled across the sky. If only her attraction to Josh could cool off as easily.

He sat on one of the stools at the island, his head in his hands. "Yes. It was *Colleen,* you know."

She'd realized that after the initial shock of hearing a female McClintock voice and thinking that Molly was about to catch them. She understood Josh's actions—he was hurting. So he either needed a balm for his ego and heart or he was lashing out at Molly and using her "second" to get back at her. But what was Brenna's excuse?

Guilt pressed against her chest as embarrassment heated her face. She'd never been one of those girls—those competitive girls who tried to steal her friends' boyfriends. While she was often bossy with her friends, she'd never been into competing.

"I realize it was Colleen," she admitted. But still she hadn't been able to face her. The girl had known her too long not to have realized that something had happened to rattle Brenna, to shake her to the core.

"What did she want?" she asked of Colleen, when she really wanted to ask the question of him, as well. What did he want? To marry Molly?

"You," he said. "She wanted to talk to you."

And instead Brenna had hidden upstairs. Her shame grew as she realized she'd betrayed two of her friends. "Was she all right?"

He shrugged. "I don't know. We talked for a while."

Brenna sighed. "She's probably so worried about Molly. She idolizes her older sister."

"I can see that. But we didn't talk about Molly."

Her breath caught. "You didn't tell her what we, about…"

"We talked about Nick."

"Nick?" She nodded. "I thought he might try to pry Molly's whereabouts out of Colleen. He has no idea how well that girl can keep a secret."

Josh grinned. "Actually, he has no idea what he's really doing."

"What do you think he's doing?"

"I think he's falling for her."

Poor Nick. Brenna, too, was learning how that felt, how out-of-control.

"What about Colleen?" She'd have to call her friend later. But she couldn't wait to talk to her. "How do you think she feels about him?"

"Wary."

"She's a smart girl," Brenna said.

"I warned her about Nick."

She tensed with concern for her friend. "Is he a womanizer?"

Josh laughed. "No, pretty much just the opposite. He's extremely careful to *not* get involved." A grin spread across Josh's face. "But I think he may not have a choice this time."

"You really think he's interested in her."

Josh nodded. "Of course, he doesn't realize that yet. Right now he's just trying to find out where Molly is."

"What would you do if you knew where Molly was?" she asked.

His eyes narrowed. "Nick was right again. Damn him. You *do* know where she is."

Unable to face Josh as she evaded the question, she lowered her gaze to the granite counter on which, just a short while ago, they'd been kissing…and more. "We're not talking about what I know."

Because she had no idea what she was thinking anymore, or why she wasn't able to suppress her attraction to her best friend's fiancé. Heck, she didn't even know why she was attracted to him at all, since he wasn't available. "What if Nick finds out and tells you?"

"Would I storm over to Eric South's and push my way inside?"

Shocked, her head shot up. "Then you know where she is."

His eyes gleamed. "Yeah."

"Did Colleen tell you?" But she doubted that her young friend would have given up her sister's whereabouts. Colleen was more loyal than Brenna had proved to be.

"*You* told me." He grinned. "Yesterday, as we headed to the dance floor, you mentioned that she might be with one friend. Since he'd backed out of being in the wedding party, Eric South was the only friend who wasn't there."

So she'd betrayed Molly even before she'd kissed Josh. "So? What are you going to do? Don't you want to talk to her?"

"Molly and I talked the night before the wedding," he reminded Brenna. "So I wasn't surprised she changed her mind about marrying me."

"You said she was having doubts, and yet you didn't call off the wedding."

He sighed. "She probably would have called off the wedding that night, if not for fear of disappointing everyone."

That sounded like Molly. "Oh…"

"She's not going to change her mind," he said. "I think she's made it clear she doesn't want to marry me."

"Why do you think that?"

"Well, if we hadn't talked the night before the wedding, I probably would have gotten my first clue when she went out the window," he said, his voice full of wry amusement rather than anger. "So whatever Molly wants time to think about, I doubt that it's me. The wedding-that-wasn't," he said, "is clearly the wedding-that-will-never-be."

Brenna shook her head, unwilling to accept that things were really over between the groom and his intended bride. "She probably just got cold feet. She may come back and want to marry you."

"But I don't want to marry her now."

"You're just mad," she insisted, although she could find no trace of anger in his voice or on his face.

"I'm not mad." He pushed his hand through his hair, and then ran it over the back of his neck. "I don't love her."

She furrowed her brow, unable to comprehend. "But why did you ask her to marry you, then?"

"Molly's a great person. She and I connected as if we'd known each other forever."

An ache spread through Brenna's chest. "You're sure you don't love her?"

His gaze met hers, and held. "Yes."

Hope should have lifted Brenna's spirit, but her feelings of responsibility weighed too heavily yet. *Poor Molly.*

He sighed. "So Molly did the right thing."

"At least someone has."

Josh looked at her squarely, his eyes as full of regret as her heart was. "I'm sorry," he said. "I shouldn't have…" He gestured toward the counter, where they'd kissed, and he blew out an agitated breath. "Twice now, I…"

Came on to her? She wasn't exactly crying sexual harassment. He hadn't crossed that line alone.

"I've turned into Mr. Hyde," he continued.

"What have I turned into?" Brenna wondered, her

head aching as if the frying pan had struck her, too. "You may think you don't love Molly, now that she left you at the altar. But I love her and I can't believe what *I* did. You're Molly's fiancé. I'm her best friend, her maid of *honor*."

"I'm leaving," he said. That would be best for both of them, even though he hated to disappoint the boys again.

"You're going back to Grand Rapids?"

"No." He shook his head. "We're not going back."

He was going forward. He hoped. He would put aside his crazy fantasy of happily-ever-after. That might work for other people, such as his folks, and hopefully even for Nick and Colleen. He only screwed things up. He was not going to attempt the third strike, when he was already out. "I called my Realtor to see if I could move into the house early."

"Of course," Brenna said, "those homes are going up fast on the outskirts of town. The builder probably doesn't need the whole two weeks to finish it."

"I didn't buy a new house." Although it probably would have made more sense if he had. But Nick had insisted on a new building for their office. For his home, Josh had wanted something with substance and character.

"You didn't?" Her brow furrowed. "What house did you buy, then?"

"The Mannings' place. It's not far from here." In fact, it was probably too damned close. "Just a street over, isn't it?"

She nodded as her face grew pale. "Yes."

Obviously she thought it was too close as well.

"I know it needs some work," he admitted. But he'd fallen for the sprawling brick ranch house the same way he'd fallen for Cloverville, seeing it as a great place to raise his boys. "I had it inspected, though, and there's nothing structurally wrong with it. I'll just have to make some cosmetic changes. I should be able to handle all the repairs myself." And working on the house would keep his hands— and his mind—off Brenna. He hoped.

"Of course," she said, her voice turned slightly cool. "Cosmetic work is what you do."

His choice of profession had been disparaged before. He'd even heard a few comments last night, from the hardware store owner—something about his being the doctor who made folks "pretty." So he was used to being patronized. But from Brenna, the comment stung. "Hey!"

"That's your job and it pays you well," she continued. "It's how you managed to outbid me on that house. That's *my* house, Josh!"

Her mama wasn't the only dramatic one in the Kelly family. He chuckled at her outrage, preferring it to her self-recrimination and guilt. "You bid on my house?"

"My house," she repeated. "But it was too late. The Mannings had already accepted a higher bid. *Yours.*"

He lifted his hands, palms up. "Why would you bid on my house? *This* is your house."

"This is my parents' house."

He shrugged. "So?"

"Do you live with your parents?"

"Of course not. For one thing, they live in Detroit, and I live in Grand… I live *here.*" He grinned. "In Cloverville."

"Yeah, in my house."

"My house," he repeated, unable to suppress a triumphant grin. "I don't understand why you wanted it."

"Why wouldn't I?" she asked, her irritation growing. Brenna was not nearly as amused with their exchange as he appeared to be.

"Your folks are great, and they dote on you. Why would you want to leave them?"

"I'm twenty-six years old. It's time I move out on my own."

"You'll break their hearts," he said.

"I left home before, for college. I shouldn't have moved back in with them when I came home. But I'd been more focused on the bakery then, and on expanding the business." And now she had time to focus on her personal life. But the two things she wanted—the house and the man— were already taken. It didn't matter that Josh claimed he didn't want Molly anymore. Not if Molly wanted him.

"Well, there are other houses," Josh remarked, as if he suddenly had qualms about having outbid her. "That new subdivision you pointed out is full of houses for sale. My Realtor took me through a few of them."

"But I wanted *that* house." Otherwise if she came home jet-lagged she was liable to walk into the wrong house since the new ones all looked the same. And she'd loved that the brick ranch was so different from her parents' house, with its small rooms and narrow halls. The Manning house was wide open. But it was not for her.

"You can see it," he offered, "with me. I'm meeting the Realtor to pick up the keys."

"The Mannings moved out early?"

"They said they've taken everything they wanted. I offered to clean out the rest."

Apparently he'd rather clean up after others than stay with her. "What about the boys?" she asked.

"I called Pop's cell. They're having ice cream right now, so they'll be a while yet."

"Okay." She nodded her agreement. After all, the Realtor would be there with them. It wasn't as though they'd be alone again. "I'll go upstairs and grab my purse. In fact, I should probably drive myself over there, in case you want to stay longer." The less time they spent together the better.

"Oh," he said. "Brenna?"

An odd note in his voice stopped her midturn, her pulse quickening. She peered back at him over her shoulder. "Yes?"

"I do have something of yours," he said.

"Yeah, the house…"

He lifted his hand, and something green and silky dangled from his index finger. Her bra.

Heat rushed to her face as embarrassment overwhelmed her. "Oh, my God! Did Colleen see it?"

How would she explain? How would she ever look at either of the McClintock sisters again?

He shook his head. "I don't think so."

"I hope you're right." She bit her lip then reached for her undergarment.

But he pulled it back, and in his deep blue eyes she glimpsed the memory of what they'd done—and what they would have done, if not for Colleen's interrupting them.

"It's your house," she conceded.

He needed it more than she did. He needed to get out before they did the something crazy with each other that Nick had alluded to.

FORTUNATELY THE HOUSE had a circular drive, allowing room for all three cars—the Realtor's, Josh's and Brenna's, plus a few more, if anyone else drove up. Josh loved the way the house sat back from the road, giving the boys a safe place to ride their bikes and roller blade. In fact, he loved everything about his new home—most especially that Brenna Kelly had wanted it, too.

"It's a good house," he said, with a satisfied nod as he opened her car door. Brenna drove an all-wheel-drive station wagon, a safe and sensible vehicle for Michigan's unpredictable winters. Josh would have expected no less of her.

Kicking aside her long skirt, she joined him on the driveway and turned toward the brick house. With a wistful sigh she admitted, "That's what I thought."

"It's a wonderful home for a family," Mrs. Applewhite said as she rushed up to join them, her high heels clicking against the cement drive. "It has great square footage and such a fabulous yard."

Josh had already bought the house, but apparently the woman couldn't stop selling.

"You won't regret your husband buying it," Mrs. Applewhite told Brenna. "Congratulations on your new home, Mrs. Towers."

"Uh, do you have the keys?" Josh asked, unwilling to correct the woman and receive yet another pitying look when he admitted that he hadn't actually married *anyone*.

"Oh," the Realtor said as she fumbled inside her briefcase. "I must have left the keys in the car. I'll be right back," she promised as she hurried over to her foreign sports car.

"You should have corrected her," Brenna said, blushing with embarrassment. "I'm not Mrs. Towers."

"Apparently Mrs. Applewhite shares my views on the similarities between marriage and duels," Josh teased her, "and she thinks you've assumed the duties of the bride." He wished she would—especially the honeymoon duties. He couldn't close his eyes, for the image of Brenna, bare to the waist, that kept flashing through his mind, testing his control and tensing every muscle in his body.

Anger flushed Brenna's face a darker red and brightened her green eyes. "I am *not* Molly's second."

No, she wasn't. Brenna Kelly was second to no one. "I know." Before he could apologize for offending her, the Realtor returned.

Mrs. Applewhite jangled the keys in her hand. "Here we are!"

Josh reached for the keys, but the blond saleswoman shook her head. "Let me get the door," Mrs. Applewhite insisted, "so you can carry your bride over the threshold."

"I'm sorry to have to correct you," Josh began. But before he could finish "correcting" her, Brenna clutched his arm, sinking her nails into the skin that was left bare by the rolled-up sleeves of his shirt.

"Wait…" Brenna interrupted him.

This woman catapulted Brenna back to high school, reminding her of all the cheerleaders who had taunted her for being overweight, calling her "fatso" and saying she'd forever be a lonely virgin. Brenna had believed them for a while… Until she learned that most men preferred women with curves. Of course there had been some guys over the years who'd changed their minds, after they'd asked her out, and had left her waiting for a date who'd never shown. Good thing she'd never minded eating alone.

For a brief moment, when Brenna had stepped from the car, surprise and then begrudging respect had crossed Mrs. Applewhite's face at the thought of Brenna landing someone as handsome and successful as Dr. Joshua Towers. Brenna didn't want the pity and condescension she was certain to see if Josh told the woman the truth. After what had nearly happened between the two of them, she couldn't handle it. She might snap the little blond Barbie in half.

"What?" both Josh and the Realtor asked her.

She opened her mouth, but the lie caught in her throat. She couldn't claim Josh as hers. She didn't have that right. "He's not my husband," she said, the words rushing out. "I was the maid of honor, not the bride."

Mrs. Applewhite's smooth forehead, probably a product of Botox, didn't furrow, but her eyebrows almost imperceptibly lifted. Was she one of Josh's patients? Was that how he'd found this woman? If he were Nick, what would he call her? Face-lift?

"Oh, I'm sorry," the woman stammered. "I just assumed. I shouldn't have. Of course *you two* aren't together like that…"

It was Brenna's turn to lift an eyebrow. "And, why is *that?*"

Because Mrs. Applewhite thought Josh too good, too perfect, for someone like Brenna? Someone *real?* The snobby woman should have seen them earlier, on the granite island in the middle of Pop and Mama's kitchen. Brenna didn't intend to share that with Mrs. Applewhite—that most men preferred women with curves.

The woman's face flushed. "I—I didn't mean…I just… you drove separately, and newlyweds usually can't be separated. Especially on their honeymoon." Her blush deepened as realization dawned, and she turned toward Josh. "So your bride…"

Josh shook his head.

"Oh, there was no…"

"Nope," he said, as though completely unconcerned, "there was no wedding." He plucked the keys from the woman's outstretched hand. "Thanks for meeting us here. We'll just let ourselves in." He jangled the keys in Brenna's directions. "After all, it is *my* house."

A smile pulled at her lips. "Only because your bid was higher." And first. She shrugged. "I guess baked goods can't compete with Botox and boob jobs."

A breath of surprise hissed out of the other woman's plump lips. Collagen, too? "I guess I'll just leave you alone then," she said, clearly perplexed by their relationship. She wasn't the only one. She turned toward Josh. "If you need anything…"

"I'll call," Josh promised.

Something flickered in her eyes—interest, perhaps as she realized that Dr. Towers was still single? "Please call," she urged him, and as she turned to walk to her car, she swung her narrow hips.

"Isn't she married?" Brenna asked, biting back a smile as the woman's heel caught in a crack in the driveway. The woman tugged her leg, pulling the heel free and continuing toward her car paying more attention to where she was walking than how she looked to Josh.

"Who?" he asked, his attention on the keys that were laying in his palm.

"*Mrs.* Applewhite. Isn't she married?"

Josh shrugged as if he was used to married women hitting on him, which he probably was. Maybe that was why Molly had gotten cold feet about marrying him. She'd envisioned a life with Josh in which she'd have to fight off all the other women who wanted him.

Brenna didn't intend to be one of those women. What had happened at her house would never happen again. Molly had seen him first. She'd dated him. She'd accepted his proposal. It didn't matter to Brenna that her friend hadn't married him—he still belonged to Molly.

Metal clanked against metal as Josh clutched the keys in his hand. Brenna turned toward him, expecting the teasing glint in his striking blue eyes. Instead his gaze was hard and his jaw was clenched.

"What's wrong?" she asked.

Chapter Eight

Everything. Emotion overwhelmed Josh. Nothing had turned out as he'd imagined it when he'd bought the house. He shoved the key into the lock, and the door creaked open—to a huge mess of left-behind trash. He wasn't surprised by the mess. He'd known the house needed work—all cosmetic and nothing structural. He'd also known that his relationship with Molly had needed work, if they were to make a success of their marriage. But he hadn't been given the opportunity. Again.

"You didn't have to tell her," he remarked. He hadn't minded Mrs. Applewhite's thinking Brenna was his bride. It actually felt right.

She shrugged her shoulders. "I thought about letting her believe…whatever the hell she wanted. But…"

"But?"

She laughed. "Hey, I did you a favor. If you'd tried to carry me over the threshold, you would have broken your back."

"Let's see," Josh proposed, as he reached for her and scooped her up into his arms.

"Put me down!" Brenna protested, but instead of pushing him away, she clutched at his shoulders, holding him closer. Her soft body molded against his. Two steps across the threshold, Josh set her down in the foyer, among the half-empty boxes and garage bags. If only she'd been his bride.

"See. You couldn't handle me," she taunted. "I'm too much woman for you."

He reached for her again, but this time Brenna stepped back until the wall stopped her retreat. Josh followed, trapping her between his body and the wall. His chest brushed against hers. "I can handle you," he promised. But maybe he lied. Maybe she *was* too much woman for him.

"Josh…"

He lowered his head until his mouth was just inches from hers. Her breath feathered across his lips. He could almost taste her. "Brenna…"

"Daddy!"

"Daddy!" the boys called out as they crashed through the open front door.

Josh stepped back from Brenna and drew in a shaky breath as he turned to greet his sons. He couldn't rush into another relationship and risk disappointing them again.

"Hey, guys!" he said.

"Is this our new house?" TJ asked, his head, swiveling as he checked out the living room.

Biting his lip to suppress a grin over his son's horrified expression—wide eyes, open mouth—Josh nodded. "What do you think?"

Buzz wrinkled his small button nose. "It stinks."

Josh could not argue that point, as the stench of moldy food drifted toward them from garbage bags strewn around the living room. There were also various stains on the carpet, and the clumps of dog hair in the corners and under where the couch must have sat in front of the tall windows.

He knew the boys couldn't imagine it as he did, with a tree house in the back, built into the ancient oak that shaded the entire yard. Tree house… No, it would be a fort. His boys would love that.

"It's messy," TJ said, "and you yell at us when our rooms are messy."

Josh snorted. "I don't yell at you, guys. I *reason* with you."

"Raisin?" Buzz asked. "All they do is stick to my teeth. They make your face turn red like it did when TJ flushed your cell phone."

TJ jabbed his elbow in his brother's ribs. "You flushed it."

"No, I put it in the *toilet,*" Buzz clarified. "*You* flushed."

"Yeah," TJ agreed. "That was when the raisin made Daddy's face turn red."

A noise spilled from Brenna's pressed-together lips— one that sounded suspiciously like a laugh. Josh shot her a glare before turning back to the boys.

"Don't worry about how the house looks now," he said, directing the conversation away from raisins and his face. "We're going to clean it up," he promised. "And after we do that, we're going to *keep* it clean."

Buzz and TJ exchanged a look, and then their faces contorted as, in unison, they grimaced. They were obviously not on board with Daddy's plan.

"We want to see our room," TJ said, speaking for both twins as they took off at a run through the living room, dodging trash spread across the worn carpet. Underneath the stained and smelly broadloom were hardwood floors that actually weren't in bad shape. Josh had checked them out the first time he'd looked at the house.

"You can each have your own bedroom," he called after them. The house had four, with room in the finished walk-out basement for more. Josh had wanted a big house, a big family, since he'd grown up as Brenna had—as an only child.

Her parents walked through the door just then. Obviously the boys had run inside the house the minute they'd stopped the car. But the Kellys had taken their time, gathering up the buckets of cleaning supplies they now carried into the living room. Pop dropped his bucket onto the floor and slung an arm around Josh's shoulders. "Son, I'm glad you bought the Manning house," he said, his face beaming with pride, as if Josh really was his son. "It's a great house."

"Isn't it a great house?" Mrs. Kelly asked her daughter.

Brenna's face flushed, probably with exasperation again over Josh's successful outbidding. "Yeah, it's a great house," she dutifully repeated.

"And it's close to ours," Mama said. "So we can see the boys as often as we like." She clutched Brenna's arm, pulling her daughter to her side. "And you can see Josh."

Josh fought a grin at her mother's obvious matchmaking. What had she and Pop seen? Josh carrying her over the threshold? Obviously Brenna thought so, as she shot him a glare.

The boys ran back into the living room, saving Brenna from having to say anything. "Someone colored all over the walls," TJ said, as if he'd never done it himself—and as if he wouldn't again the minute Josh painted them.

"And the kitchen really stinks," Buzz said. "There's food in the fridge."

"And it's fuzzy," TJ added.

Josh lifted his hands to hold off their complaints. "We'll clean it up, I promise. We'll start with the living room. Then we can sleep in here tonight—in sleeping bags. It'll be like we're camping out."

"Let's camp outside," TJ said.

"It stinks in here," Buzz said yet again, obsessing over the pungent odor. Not that Josh could blame him. The house hadn't been this dirty the first time the Realtor had shown it to him. Maybe he should have given the Mannings two more weeks for cleanup.

Thunder rumbled in the distance. The clouds were so thick and dark outside that it looked as if evening had come early. Despite all the windows, Josh needed to turn on some lights.

"No one's sleeping outside," Mama declared. "You're staying with us until you get this house all ready for you and the boys."

Josh shook his head. "It's not that bad," he insisted. "We can clean it up ourselves."

"No!" Buzz shouted. "We didn't make the mess."

"We're not cleaning it up!" TJ took up their tag-team argument.

"We'll *all* clean it up," Brenna offered.

Pop grabbed a hold of a cleaning bucket and rattled the contents. "We came with supplies."

"You didn't have to do that," Josh said. When he had called the older man on his cell phone, he'd explained that he was taking possession of the house early because he'd offered to clean up after the Mannings. "I hope I didn't give you the impression I was asking you for help."

"In Cloverville, you don't have to *ask* for help," Pop explained.

Like Buzz, Mama wrinkled her nose as she glanced down at the carpet. "It's going to take more than a good cleaning to make this house livable," she observed. "The carpets need to go right away. And everything has to be painted." She turned to Josh, her eyes sparkling. "You and the twins will be staying with us for a while."

Brenna, her face even paler than before, shook her head. "That won't be necessary," she told her mother, with a pointed glance. "We'll get a town work bee going. Like Josh said, the house is not that bad. He'll be able to move in soon."

And out of her life? Obviously she wanted to get rid of him, and he couldn't blame her.

BRENNA GLANCED AT HER WATCH. She needed to be at the office, especially on a Monday morning, and especially as she'd already taken off Friday to help her parents with the rehearsal dinner and last-minute details for the wedding-that-wasn't. Of course she had more-than-competent bakery managers and office staff. They could handle things for another day, and maybe even for the rest of the week. All she really had to do was check in to handle emergencies.

Because she'd rather be there in the park. With *him*... and his brother.

"You didn't tuck us in last night," Buzz whined, his lower lip sticking out.

"You're a sissy girl," TJ hurled the insult at his twin.

"No, you're a sissy girl," Buzz shot back as he scrambled up from the grass and chased TJ across the park.

"Goodbye," Mama called out, waving as she headed toward her car, which was parked behind Brenna's at the curb. The boys were Brenna's responsibility now.

She bit her lip to hold back a smile. She'd skipped tucking them in the night before, not wanting to intrude on their bedtime ritual with their father. Not wanting to see their father again. But still, instead of going to the office, she'd driven to the park, where Mama had said she was taking them that morning.

TJ ran up to her and flung his arms around her neck. "You should've said good-night," he cried out, adding his complaint to his brother's.

She pulled him close for a tight hug and smacked her lips against his cheek. He cuddled with her for half a minute before wriggling loose. Then Buzz took his turn, launching himself into her arms. She smacked a kiss against *his* cheek, then blew raspberries into his neck. He giggled and squirmed free. "Brenna!"

How had she resisted them even for one night? No wonder, instead of going in to the bakery as she'd planned, she'd stopped here. The minute she'd opened her door, she'd heard the squeals and shouts as they played an energetic game of tag. She'd been tagged *It* before she realized they'd even noticed her. Of course they hadn't made the game much of a challenge since she'd dropped onto the grass, heedless of her slacks and flowered blouse, and the boys kept running up to her.

"Who's It now?" TJ asked.

"You're both It," Brenna said, "but we're going to stop playing and go over to your new house to start working. Pop dropped off a Dumpster…"

"What's a Dumpster?"

"A big metal garbage can. You had your pop-fight behind one at the party," she reminded them. "And you're going to help your dad fill this one with all the junk the old owners left in the house."

"It smells bad in there," Buzz said. "I wanna stay here and play."

"Your dad needs your help," Brenna insisted. It was just

him and the boys. And she suspected it might stay that way, since Molly had yet to come home.

Brenna had called Abby that morning, over at the McClintocks, and her friend had verified the fact. Molly had to be with Eric. Ever since he'd moved to Cloverville, he had been the one Molly had turned to. Brenna had also called Colleen, at the insurance agency where she worked for Clayton, and she hadn't seen her sister, either—or so she'd claimed.

"You're It," TJ shouted as he touched her shoulder and then ran off with his brother.

With a groan, Brenna scrambled to her feet. "I don't run," she shouted after them.

Giggling, they scrambled into the bushes surrounding the statue of the town founder, Colonel Clover. Then screams replaced the giggles as they fell over each other, in their hurry to get out. Both of them ran back to her and buried their faces against her sides.

Her heart beating fast, she patted their trembling backs. "What's wrong? Are you all right?"

"There's s-something in there," Buzz stammered.

"An animal?" She ran her gaze over both of them, checking for teeth marks. But they bore only scratches from the branches. "Did something bite you?"

"No…" TJ whimpered. "It's a-a-a…"

"Head," Buzz said on a gasp.

Brenna swung her gaze back to the statue. Sure enough the old colonel had lost his head again. He'd been the victim of a drive-by eight years earlier, and the town, and specifically the thrifty mayor, Mr. Carpenter, had decided it wouldn't dole out the money required to have the statue properly welded back together. "It's just metal," she assured the boys. "It's not real."

They lifted their faces and stared up at her. "Really?"
She nodded.

"It's cool," Buzz said more calmly.

"Yeah, cool."

A couple of Brenna's friends didn't share that opinion.
Few people knew that Colleen had been the one behind the
wheel of the car with the bad brakes that had accidentally
hit the colonel. She'd been only fifteen at the time and intent on running away. Since it had been Abby's car, Abby
had insisted on taking the blame, believing, and rightfully
so, that the town would blame her anyway. Of course
Brenna didn't know this for certain, as Abby and Colleen
had kept the truth a secret since then.

Goose bumps rose on the boys' bare arms. "It's getting
cool out here," Brenna observed. June in western Michigan
was unpredictable; it could be as warm as summer or as
chilly as winter. Today it was just like early spring, with a
brisk breeze and a smattering of clouds. "Let me get you
to your dad before he worries."

Mama had promised she'd bring them over to the house
when they'd finished breakfast. Josh, himself, must have
left at dawn, obviously determined to get some work done.

Brenna buckled the boys into the back of her station
wagon and drove the few streets over to the house that
should have been hers. The minute she stopped the car, the
twins jumped out and ran around to the overgrown backyard. Sighing, she followed them—at a much slower pace.

"I'm sure your dad is working on the yard last," she
pointed out. "We need to get inside."

TJ, jumping up to try to reach a tree branch, said,
"Daddy doesn't need our help. Uncle Nick is here."

That was whose sleek red sports car was parked behind

Josh's family-size SUV, next to the Dumpster Pop had had dropped in front of the garage.

"Well, you still need to help your dad. Then, once you're done cleaning up, you can start painting your room."

"Daddy said we can't help paint," Buzz whined as he tried to stretch his arms around the ancient oak tree.

"Cuz we'll make a mess," TJ added.

The house was already a mess, and if Josh intended to use only the white paint, several cans of which she'd noticed in the back of his SUV as she'd run after the boys, the twins wouldn't be able to do much damage. Not with that boring sterile color. Recognizing that they weren't ready to start working yet, she dropped onto the lawn, which was more weeds than grass.

"I don't wanna move here," Buzz whined again as he ran back to her and dropped onto her lap. "I wanna live with you."

TJ abandoned his quest for the branch, ran back and dropped down beside his brother. He elbowed Buzz aside for more room. "Me, too. I wanna stay with you and Mama and Pop."

"Your daddy bought this house, so that you can live *here*. All of you." And Molly. He'd bought this house—*her* house—for Molly. For her best friend. If Molly came back, he might resume that future with her for whatever his reason, since he claimed love hadn't been a factor.

"If *we* have to live here," Buzz lamented, "then we want you to live here, too."

"Live with us!" TJ added.

"Then you could tuck us in every night," Buzz murmured.

Brenna wrapped her arms around both boys and sprayed raspberries against their cheeks. "You sure you want me slobbering all over you?"

They squirmed and giggled, but neither tried to break free of her. Brenna was the one who wanted to run—screaming—from all the Towers males, big and little.

"YOU *BOUGHT* THIS PLACE?" Nick asked as he stepped over the threshold over which Josh had carried Brenna the day before. "You *really* bought this place?"

Josh nodded and smiled at his friend's shocked reaction. Maybe he should have left Nick in the garage—he'd already cleaned up most of it with Nick's grudging help. "It's a great house."

"It's a dump," Nick insisted as he explored the H-shaped layout. The kitchen, family room, mud room and half bath were behind the two-stall garage, a formal living and dining area was in the middle, and a wing of four bedrooms and three baths was on the far side.

Josh grinned as he followed his friend through each room. "I love it."

Nick turned and looked at him as if he'd lost his mind. And Josh probably had. But at least he had something physical to do, some way of burning off the sexual energy that was humming through his body.

"You're crazy. You thought your bride would like this place?" he asked. "Really?"

Brenna Kelly did. "I don't know…" Josh hadn't really thought about Molly when he'd bought the house. He'd only thought of what a great house and yard this would be for the boys and the other kids he wanted to have some day.

"Have you heard from her?" Nick asked.

"Who?"

"Your runaway bride—has she called?" Nick asked. "Stopped by? Anything?"

Josh shook his head. "Nope."

"What about *her?*" he asked, gesturing toward where Brenna played in the backyard with the boys.

Josh's chest muscles tightened. He'd thought Brenna had been going in to the office, just for the morning, before she came by the house to help. And now she, instead of Mama, had his children. She looked so damn natural with them, as if they were her sons, too.

Clearing his throat, he asked, "What about Brenna?"

"Did *she* hear from her friend?"

He shrugged. "I don't know."

"Did you ask?" Nick persisted.

Josh shook his head.

"Do you care?"

"What?"

"Do you care what happened to your runaway bride?" Nick asked, staring through the French doors to the backyard, as Josh did. "Or do you care more about *her?*"

Josh pulled his gaze from Brenna. "I don't know what you're talking about."

Nick nodded. "Sure you do. *You* just don't want to talk about it—about *her*—yet. We've known each other too long, man."

"Yeah, we have." Josh knocked his shoulder against Nick's. "So tell me, did Colleen show up for your little picnic?"

Color flushed Nick's face. "Colleen?"

"That's the bridesmaid *you're* working on, right? To find out where Molly is?" he persisted.

"It's not like that," Nick said defensively. "I'm not using Colleen. I wouldn't do that to her."

Josh nodded. "No, you're not using her. You're falling for her." He wouldn't have believed it if he hadn't seen it himself—the excitement and affection in Nick's eyes at just the mention of Colleen McClintock's name.

Nick snorted. "You're the one who falls for women five minutes after you meet them. Not me," he vehemently insisted.

Was that what Josh was doing with Brenna? Falling for her? He cleared his throat and changed the subject. "Okay, enough stalling. Let's get back to work so we can finish cleaning this place and start painting."

Nick didn't argue the subject change, but whistled at Josh's ambition. "Why are you in such a hurry to get this dump livable? I thought you had a place to stay."

Josh cleared his throat. If he stayed much longer with Brenna Kelly, he'd wind up as crazy as his best friend feared he would become. "Yeah, but this is my house," he said, "and I really want to make it a home for the boys."

Brenna blinked to clear the mist from Josh's image. God, the man couldn't be any more perfect. The perfect father, the perfect friend. To resist the attraction, she had to find some fault with him. She had to be tough. So she said, "Then don't mess it up."

The two men whirled toward her, obviously unaware that she'd overheard the end of their conversation. "Mess it up?" Josh asked.

"You may have outbid me, but I'll find a way to take the house away from you…" she threatened "…if you use that boring paint you bought."

"What's wrong with the paint?" Josh asked. "I bought it from Mr. Carpenter's hardware store like Pop told me to."

"That was smart," she said. "If you want to fit in in

Cloverville, you have to support the local businesses. The ones that have always been part of Cloverville."

"We haven't always been part of Cloverville," Nick pointed out, "so we're going to be lucky to get any business at the new office."

"If you try to fit in, they'll eventually trust you," Brenna assured him.

"Eventually," Nick muttered. "Great, just great."

"We've been supporting the local bakery," Josh said, pointing toward the box of doughnuts. "Of course, Pop won't let me pay for anything…"

Brenna sighed. "That's why I had to take over the bakery." To secure her parents' retirement, although she sometimes doubted they ever intended to retire. Maybe once she gave them those grandkids they kept hinting about…

Nick bit into the doughnut he pulled from the box. "Mmm. You're doing a great job." Then he saluted her with a bear claw, a sweet roll covered with nuts and caramel icing. "Now, what about the paint?"

"Yeah, what's wrong with the paint?" Josh asked.

"It's white," Brenna said, disgusted by the doctors' lack of imagination. But then even though Josh was the perfect man, he was still a man.

Josh nodded. "Yeah?" Both men appeared clueless.

"It's all white," she said.

"What's wrong with that?" Josh asked. "Nick, tell her there's nothing wrong with white."

"Of course you two would be fine with that. You're doctors." She smiled, as if unimpressed, even though she had much respect for their chosen profession.

"So?" Josh prodded her.

"You like cold and sterile," she explained.

"It's not cold and sterile."

"I'll let you handle this argument," Nick said, patting his friend's shoulder in silent support. "Let me see if the boys want something to eat."

"Don't get them all hyped up on sugar," Josh cautioned.

But his best friend stepped through the French doors, brandishing the box as if he hadn't heard a word Josh had said. "Damn…"

"They'll wear off the sugar while they're helping clean," she promised.

"Clean? You *have* met my sons, right?" he checked. "They don't pick up their toys, their clothes, their gum wrappers… Nothing."

"Well, then it's past time they learned."

"Buzz and TJ?" He widened his eyes. "They've been suspended from *preschool* for not following the rules."

Somehow she suspected he wasn't kidding. Yet she couldn't help but laugh. "Okay, but you need to have them do some work on the house, too, so that they'll feel like they're helping you make this their home."

Josh narrowed his eyes. "So you're giving me parenting advice?"

Heat rose to her face. "I know I have no right…" But having no right hadn't stopped her from kissing him.

"Wow," he mused, his eyes twinkling again, "I've flustered Brenna Kelly."

It wasn't the first time. "What…?"

"I thought you were totally in charge at all times."

"I think we both know better than that," she said, closing her eyes on a memory of the two of them.

"We need to talk about *that,*" Josh said.

"No, we don't," she insisted. "We need to talk about the paint."

"So you're a decorator as well as a parenting expert?" he said, his eyes losing some of their sparkle.

"I took some extra classes at college," she admitted.

"Interior design?"

One course in interior design. And another in child psychology. She'd always intended to get married and have kids, but she'd wanted the bakery to be a success first. She hadn't realized that if she waited too long someone else would take the house she wanted and her best friend would get the guy…

She nodded. "Yes."

"I suppose you have paint colors all picked out for *my* house?"

"Of course," she said, as if he should have known. "I even bought the paint."

His eyes widened. "You bought the paint? Kind of getting ahead of yourself, weren't you?"

"This house had been for sale for a while before I started looking. I had no idea someone else had put in a bid just before me."

"So what colors were you planning to paint *my* house?" he asked.

She walked around the living room, envisioning her colors on the dingy walls. "In the formal living room, and dining room a deep chocolate. Sage, in the kitchen and family room."

"Sage?"

"You know—a grayish-green."

He nodded. "I know what color it is, but why would you put that in the kitchen?"

"It's sage." During that decorating class, she'd given a lot of thought to the colors she'd paint her own house one day.

"With that carpet?"

"There's ceramic tile under that carpet," she reminded him. "I pulled up a corner of it." She gestured toward the worn and stained yellow broadloom on the living room floor. "And hardwood in here."

"Yeah, I know." He glanced around as if considering her choices. Then he shook his head. "White will brighten everything up and make it clean—like a fresh start."

A fresh start. Now she understood his move to Cloverville. He had wanted a fresh start for him and Molly.

Ignoring the pang of jealousy that she had no right to feel she continued her paint argument, even though she had no more right to the house than the man. "Let some color into your life, Josh. Go for it!"

He stepped closer. "And here I thought you wanted me to back off."

Brenna drew a shaky breath, but she refused to back away this time and planted her bare feet on the floor. She'd left her canvas sandals in the backyard with the boys. Without them Josh seemed to tower over her. Tall, dark and handsome.

Her breath caught in her lungs. "I do want you to back off," she insisted. "I can't… You and I, we can't… Molly is my best friend. She has been since we were nearly the same age as the twins."

"Molly doesn't want to marry me," Josh insisted. "She made that clear when she failed to show up at the church."

"She was at the church."

"Well, she failed to show at the altar."

"After she has some time alone to think, she'll change

her mind," Brenna insisted. Molly was too smart *not* to change her mind.

He sighed. "It doesn't matter if *Molly* changes her mind."

"It doesn't matter," she agreed. Because Molly had had him first. So if, as he'd sworn, he didn't want to marry Molly anymore, it didn't matter to Brenna. She still couldn't be *hers.* She shook off her disappointment and focused instead on what else she'd lost without ever really having it. "What matters is that you don't paint this house boring white."

He touched her hair, sliding a lock between his fingertips. "I'm beginning to see the wisdom of color. Maybe I should paint the whole house red."

"Red would be too much," she said. "Way more than you could handle."

He dipped his head, his mouth a breath way from hers. "But I like red."

"I thought you'd prefer the brown."

He shook his head. "No, someone suggested that I need more color in my life."

Was he saying he needed *her?*

Brenna's pulse quickened. "Josh…"

His lips touched hers, brushing back and forth. She needed to pull back, she needed to step away. But her legs went limp and she could barely stand, let alone walk.

Josh was the one to step back and to release her.

"What…?" she asked, lifting her hands toward his shoulders. That soft, brief kiss, that wasn't enough. Not when she knew there was so much more passion between them.

Chapter Nine

Josh caught her hands in his and pulled them away from him, his heart heavy with regret. If only he hadn't heard the car drive up and the voices drifting in from the driveway.

But if someone hadn't driven up, Nick and the boys probably would have interrupted them. Actually, with Nick and the boys there, Josh hadn't intended to be alone with Brenna. He hadn't *wanted* to be alone with Brenna. Because he wanted her…

"Josh?" She called his name, her green eyes registering both passion and confusion.

He gestured toward the front door, on which someone had just knocked.

"I don't understand why I have to help him out," Rory McClintock griped as he entered the house.

"He was almost your brother-in-law," Mrs. McClintock explained. "He may still be, when Molly comes home."

Did he detect a note of disappointment in his almost-mother-in-law's voice? Perhaps she was the one who'd helped Molly come to her senses.

"Molly's not here," the teenager muttered, "so why do I have to be?"

"Because you're out of school for the summer, and this is your detention for spiking the punch bowl at the wedding. You're Dr. Towers's manual labor."

Or was she punishing Josh?

"I thought *I* was the manual labor," Nick said as he stepped through the French doors.

Actually, what Nick was supposed to have been was the chaperone Josh had wanted so that he didn't do what he'd already done—kiss Brenna Kelly again.

"You're not getting out of working," Josh warned his friend. But he wouldn't need Nick for a chaperone, not when he had Rory and his mother.

The kid had probably been right, back in the limo, when he'd said Josh was lucky for not marrying into the McClintock family. They had the worst timing.

Brenna, her face flushed with the sort of color she'd boldly told him he needed in his life, stood near Mrs. McClintock. Her gaze was focused on the floor, however, and not on the woman she'd known since childhood. "Have you heard from Molly?" she asked.

Mrs. McClintock, with dark curly hair like her son's and the McClintock legacy of dark eyes, slung an arm around Brenna's shoulders. "Don't worry about Molly," she told the maid of honor. "She'll be just fine. I'm sure she'll come back soon."

Then maybe Brenna would accept the fact that Josh and her friend were not in love and never getting married. But it shouldn't matter to Josh that she believed him. The last thing he wanted was to jump from an engagement/almost marriage into another relationship.

No, the McClintocks' arrival had been perfectly timed, saving him from making another mistake that could have cost him his heart—and the sanity over which Nick was so concerned. He had to focus on his children and his house, and forget all about Brenna Kelly.

"I THOUGHT YOU TWO WASHED UP at the house," Brenna said as she steered the boys to the restroom in the back of the bakery. They still had more paint on *them* than on the walls of Josh's house. And so did Nick, thanks to Josh teaching his boys how to tease his friend by flicking paint into his hair.

Uncle Nick could not have handled the boys for two weeks, not by himself. But then with the way he acted whenever anyone brought up Colleen's name, maybe he wouldn't have had to handle them alone. Josh was probably right. His friend was falling for the youngest McClintock sister.

"Dry your hands," she told the boys as they passed her on their way out of the bathroom. "Wait for me, too. We just stopped here to clean up." And so that Brenna could pick up her messages. She hadn't been in the office much the week before the wedding, and now she hadn't been in most of the week since the wedding-that-wasn't.

She had been too busy taking care of Molly's business, when she should have been taking care of her own. Fortunately she had a team of accomplished bakers and savvy office staff. And if Pop and Mama weren't helping Josh at the house, they were here instead—baking and handling anything else that might need immediate attention.

Brenna ran water in the sink to rinse the green paint from the white porcelain. Then she glanced in the mirror above the basin and noted a smear of paint on her face.

Had the boys done that? She flashed back to when she'd left the house, originally to take the boys back to Pop and

Mama's for a nap, and Josh had brushed a lock of hair from her cheek to tuck behind her ear. His finger had followed the exact path of the green smeared across her face.

"Damn him," she murmured as she reached for a paper towel. Nick wasn't the only one he'd played a practical joke on. She leaned closer to the mirror and checked her hair, which she'd bound into a high ponytail. At least he hadn't spattered paint in her hair, as he'd taught the boys to do with Nick.

Grunts and groans and the high-pitched screech of ripping paper reverberated in the reception area.

"Let me see!" TJ shouted.

"No, I wanna see first!" Buzz shouted back. "I found it!"

Oh, God, what had they found? Maybe she should have taken them directly home for that nap. Even though she'd thought they'd gotten a second wind the minute she'd buckled them into the backseat, they sounded overtired and cranky.

Brenna scrubbed away the paint and headed out to break up the fight. The boys wrestled over a magazine. Not a car or sports magazine, but one of the fashion ones that Brenna's assistant had fanned out across an antique chest that served as a coffee table in the comfortable but elegant reception area. Antiques that had overflowed out of the Kelly house had washed up at the bakery.

"What do you guys want to look at in this?" she asked as she put her hands over theirs on top of the glossy cover with the tattered edges, where they'd ripped it. Their pudgy fingers held the magazine open to a provocative advertisement. Weren't they too young to be looking at lingerie ads? She really needed to speak to Deb about the magazines she put out. Right now the receptionist's desk sat empty, the phone going to voice mail while she took her lunch break.

Despite their hostility toward each other, the twins exchanged one of their silent *looks*. Then TJ relinquished his grip on the magazine and spoke for them both. "We wanna see our mom."

Buzz let go, too, leaving only Brenna holding the magazine open to a page featuring the image of a scantily clad model.

"Your mom?" she asked. They'd been so young when she'd deserted them that they must have woven fantasies about who she was.

"That's her," TJ said, pointing toward the waiflike blonde in an ad for knock-off lingerie. The model looked about as real as a plastic doll.

"But I didn't think you guys were old enough to remember her when she left," she said, not wanting to hurt their feelings, but wanting to be honest with them. Had they latched on to the image of this woman as their mother just as they'd latched on to Brenna? And as they probably would have latched on to Molly if she'd married their father? They were desperate for a mother to replace the one who'd deserted them.

"We were little," TJ admitted.

"You were a baby," Buzz said.

"*You* were a baby!"

Brenna held up the magazine to stave off another argument. "So why do you think *this* is your mother?"

"Daddy said it was. And he showed us other pictures of her, too," Buzz told Brenna.

"She didn't look like that in Daddy's pictures, though. She had a big nose and dark hair. So then he showed us a magazine, so we'd know what she looks like now," TJ explained.

Buzz grabbed the magazine from Brenna's hand and hurled it against the wall. "I don't want to see her!"

Because their mother didn't want to see them. No one, not Josh or Molly or the boys, had told Brenna much about this woman. But she'd assumed the boys' mother hadn't had any contact with them since she'd left. Now Brenna knew why. The woman had been too busy building her career—one she apparently owed to Josh for helping her to look different, so she could land magazine ads.

TJ pushed his brother, knocking him to the floor. "You're not supposed to throw stuff inside. You're bad. She left because you're bad."

"You're bad!" Buzz shouted back, pummeling his brother with small fists.

Brenna knelt on the floor and pulled the boys into her arms. Elbows and knees jabbed her as they fought each other and her, but she continued to hold them close, gently but firmly. "Neither one of you is bad."

TJ hiccupped a sob. "We are. That's what all the nannies say when they quit."

"That we're bad," Buzz agreed, no longer fighting the insult.

Brenna's heart ached with their pain, with the loss of the people who'd already come and gone in their young lives. No matter what happened with Josh, she would have to maintain contact with his boys.

"You're not bad. Either one of you," she insisted, hugging them closer. "You're sweet, loving, fun, smart boys." And she'd be proud to call them her sons. She would never leave them as their mother had.

"I wish you were our mom," TJ said, hiccupping again.

Buzz rubbed his eyes, dashing away all evidence of the

tears he'd shed before his brother could call him a sissy girl. "Me, too."

She couldn't lie to them. "I wish I was, too," she admitted. "But I'm not. Maybe Molly will come home soon and she'll become your mother."

"We want you," TJ insisted.

"Would you be happy with a cookie?" she asked as she rose from the floor and pulled the boys up. "We can see if Pop and Mama will let you help out in the kitchen."

To get their minds off their mother, she took them on a tour of the bakery. At the end of the tour she left them in the kitchen with her parents, so that she could slink off to her office. Her chair creaked as she leaned over her desk. The torn and crumpled magazine, open to the picture of their mother, blurred before her eyes as tears threatened and then fell. She lifted her hands to her face and tried to stem them. But the boys' misery over their mother's abandonment filled her heart. It didn't matter that they'd been so young when she'd left—they still knew what they were missing. A mother.

Was Josh missing her, his model ex-wife, too? Was that why he'd proposed to Molly, because she was gorgeous enough to be a model?

Knuckles rapped against her doorjamb, startling Brenna. With a shaking hand she pushed the magazine beneath a stack of files and reached for a tissue.

"Hey, Brenna," called out a feminine voice, soft with concern, "are you okay?"

She closed her eyes tight then scrubbed at them with the tissue. She'd thought her assistant, Deb, back from lunch, had been the one knocking at her door—not her old friend. She lifted her gaze to Abby Hamilton. In short shorts and a white tank top, the petite blonde appeared taller than her barely five foot frame. While she leaned against the door-jamb, she was anything but casual as she intently studied Brenna's face.

"I'm fine," Brenna assured her friend.

"You've been crying."

Brenna shook her head. "PMS. Don't worry about me."

Abby's eyes narrowed with skepticism, but then, as if giving Brenna time to pull herself together, she turned her attention to the office. Brenna had painted the walls to look like Venetian plaster. Overstuffed chairs and antique oak furniture made the space as inviting as the home Brenna had hoped to someday make for herself.

Abby's quick perusal of the office finished, she returned her attention to Brenna. Her gaze suspicious, she declared, "You don't cry over PMS."

"Allergies, then…" she blithely lied "…making my eyes water."

"Brenna, I hope you know you can talk to me. I won't tell anyone."

Her heart warmed with love and respect for her friend. She hoped Abby moved home for good—she'd really missed her. E-mails, phone calls and letters were no sub-stitute for the real thing. Of course, with helping Josh on the house and with the boys, she hadn't had time to see Abby much since the wedding. "I know you'd take my secrets to your grave," Brenna said. "Colleen told me."

Colleen had told her the truth, with her inexplicable guilt more than her words. That Abby had taken the blame when Colleen had driven her car through Cloverville Park and into Colonel Clover. Everyone had believed the wild Hamilton girl had been responsible, and Abby, too, had insisted she'd been behind the wheel. Getting expelled from school had just given her a reason to leave Cloverville a little earlier than she'd been planning to leave. Which she'd been preparing for more because of her sorry excuses for parents than the town. Like Colleen, Brenna had often felt guilty, but with her it was for having so much more than Abby and Eric.

"I don't know what you're talking about," Abby insisted.

Abby, probably believing the secret was Colleen's to tell, would never admit the truth. And Brenna didn't want to talk about her tears, so she wadded up her tissue, tossed it in the trash and changed the subject. "Have you heard from Molly?"

"No. That's why I stopped by," Abby admitted, her eyes full of concern for their missing friend.

The longer Molly stayed away, the less concerned and more angry Brenna became. Even if Molly didn't intend to marry Josh, she should be the one helping him with the house and with his boys. No matter what he claimed, Brenna knew Molly was the reason Josh had decided to move to Cloverville.

"We could drive over to Eric's," she said.

"And what?" Abby asked, with a nervous laugh, as if she believed Brenna might consider her suggestion. "Break down the door?"

Her temper flaring, Brenna admitted, "I wouldn't have a problem with that."

"But they might." Molly and Eric. "And then we what… Lose *two* friends?"

Her nerves were frayed from fighting her attraction to Molly's fiancé—or ex-fiancé—and Brenna let her bitterness creep into her voice. "So you don't want to do anything? You're content to sit around and wait for her to figure out what she really wants?"

She didn't know how much longer she could fight her feelings.

"I'm never content," Abby reminded her. "I understand Molly being confused. Ever since her dad died, she's thrown herself into school and hasn't taken a minute to think."

Brenna had been there with Molly through most everything but medical school. She knew how hard Molly had pushed herself. Her anger drained away, and she sighed. "You're right. She deserves to take some time to herself for once."

"Yes," Abby agreed.

"So what are you doing today?" Brenna asked. She hoped that Abby was moving home and opening an office of her clever Temps to Go employment agency in Cloverville. But she didn't ask. She suspected Mary McClintock was already putting enough pressure on Abby, and she didn't want to add any more.

"I'm giving Lara a behind-the-scenes look at a bakery." Abby smiled, her eyes shining with love as they always did when she thought of her daughter.

Brenna stood up and peered around Abby's frame, looking for the shy, little girl. "Where is she?"

"Your parents stole her from me the minute I walked through the door."

Brenna laughed and warned her friend, "You may not get her back. They've pretty much stolen the twins from Josh."

"I thought I heard them," Abby said. Even now back in the wing of offices, peals of laughter could be heard all the way from the kitchen. "Lots of sugar might not be the best idea for them."

"They're good boys," Brenna insisted. "They've been through a lot."

Abby nodded. "I know." She adjusted her eyes again, as if scrutinizing Brenna. "Josh still staying with your family?"

Brenna nodded. "He's waiting for Molly to come back." Despite what he claimed.

"*Poor* Molly," Abby said with a smile. "Men always fall for her."

No one knew that better than Brenna. But she couldn't blame Molly for being Molly. She couldn't blame Molly for anything—Brenna was the one who had betrayed their friendship. Until Molly told her personally that she had no more interest in Josh, Brenna had no business kissing him.

Heck, even if Molly didn't want him, Brenna didn't either. She glanced down at her desk, to where a corner of the glossy magazine peeked out beneath a file for Kelly Confections. She could never compete with a lingerie model, and she had no interest in trying.

"I can't believe how much this place has changed," Abby said, gesturing around her. "You have a wonderful setup here."

Brenna settled her hip on the corner of her desk, careful not to knock over the pile of folders. A smile of honest pride formed. And she couldn't resist adding just a little pressure of her own for Abby to move back home. "See, you can run a successful business from Cloverville."

"*Et tu,* Brenna?"

She laughed. "Yes, I think you should open an office in Cloverville. I think you should stay here, and not just until Molly comes back. You should stay here for *good.* It's home."

Abby sighed. "No, Brenna, it's not."

Brenna reached out, closing her hands around Abby's

shoulders. She stared steadily into her friend's eyes, letting Abby know that she'd seen the kiss on the dance floor between the blonde and Clayton McClintock—the man Abby claimed to hate. She'd also heard about another kiss between the pair, right in front of Mr. Carpenter's hardware store on Main Street. Every townsperson who'd stopped by the house to help Josh this week had commented on how the couple hadn't been aware of anything but each other.

Abby's slender shoulders tensed beneath Brenna's hands, as if she were bracing herself for taunts or "I told you so's." But she would never purposely hurt a friend. So all Brenna offered was a bit of wisdom. "Home is where the heart is, honey."

PAINT DRIPPED from the bristles of the brush, sliding down the crease between the trim and the wall. Josh grabbed a rag, caught the drip and wiped green paint off the white trim. He hadn't envisioned spending his honeymoon like *this*. With *him*.

"Nick," he called out to his friend. "Can you believe we're almost done?" It seemed almost impossible that the entire house had been cleaned and painted in just a week. Of course, just about the entire town of Cloverville had helped out at one point or another. But especially the Kellys—and most especially, Brenna Kelly. She couldn't make it any more obvious that she wanted him out of her house.

Her parents' house, actually. She considered this her house, and he'd been very fortunate to beat her to it.

"Nick!" he called out again.

His friend pushed a dry roller against the wall, taking more of the green—sage—paint off the kitchen walls than he'd put on. He'd showed up today, but he hadn't been much more help than the boys. Only his body was present, his mind, somewhere else.

Josh suspected it was with Colleen McClintock. Biting back a grin, Josh dipped his brush into the can of paint, then flicked it so droplets spattered across Nick's face.

Nick turned his attention to the roller, which he hadn't bothered to dip in the paint for quite a while. So Josh flicked him once again. More paint drops splattered his face and slid down his neck.

Nick closed his eyes and threatened, "Hey, Buzz, I'm going to get you for that."

Maybe because Buzz was his namesake, he and Nick shared a special bond. And Buzz could never quite leave Nick alone—he constantly sought his attention.

"You better run," Nick threatened. He whirled around, as if ready to chase down his namesake.

But only Josh stood behind him, unable to entirely wipe the grin from his face.

"Where are the boys?" Nick asked.

Josh's face strained as his grin widened. "Brenna took them back to her house for naps."

"Naps?" Nick repeated, incredulous, as if he doubted they *ever* slept.

"Working on the house tires them out," Josh explained. And they had really worked, at Brenna's urging. She'd been right, too. They weren't as opposed to living here now that they'd helped turn the house into a home. But he suspected they would still struggle when it came to leaving the Kellys', where every moment was filled with food and fun.

Nick shook his head, stunned. "I didn't see them leave."

"You haven't been very aware of anything today," Josh pointed out. "I've been calling your name for a while now."

Nick shrugged. "I often ignore you, so that's nothing different."

"You are," he insisted. "You've been different since the wedding."

"The wedding-that-wasn't."

He laughed at his friend's obvious ploy to divert the conversation back to Josh. "You're not going to distract me."

"Probably not," Nick readily agreed. "I don't have red hair and big…"

Josh flicked the paintbrush again, before his friend could finish his description of Brenna Kelly. Nick blinked and wiped at his eyes and mouth. But instead of getting mad his best friend was smug, so Josh cursed him, "Damn you!"

Nick laughed. "See, I distracted you. Or was that her…"

"Who's distracting you?" Josh asked. "Or do I need to ask? Let me see. She has brown hair and big brown eyes. And an innocence and vulnerability about her that suggests she'd be easily hurt." Josh set his paintbrush on the counter, which, like the cupboards, had been covered with plastic drop cloths. "Are you going to hurt her?"

"You didn't marry her sister," Nick said, his deep voice defensive. "You're not her big brother."

Oh, Nick… When would the guy stop fighting falling in love. Josh hoped it was before Colleen got hurt, because she really was a sweet girl. "I'm her friend," he said.

"You've only just met her."

"I've known Colleen for years," he corrected Nick.

"You have?"

"From the hospital."

"You knew she volunteered?"

"You didn't?" Josh laughed. "Oh, that's right. You make it a point to never pay attention to the volunteers or the staff. Only the patients."

"It's kept my life uncomplicated," Nick pointed out. "Your life would have been better if you'd done the same."

"Easier, maybe," Josh agreed since he'd met both his brides at the hospital. "But not better. I don't regret having my sons."

"They're good kids."

Josh laughed. "I thought we'd sworn we would never lie to each other."

"No, really, they are," Nick said as if he meant it.

Josh grinned, his chest filling with pride in his children. "Yes, they are."

"The house is finally starting to shape up," Nick said as if he'd just opened his eyes.

"I'm not selling it." He—and Brenna—had worked too hard to make it a home. Too bad he couldn't share it with her. While she wanted the house, she didn't want him or his sons. Would she, if she believed Molly didn't want him?

"No, I think you should stay," Nick admitted. "This place suits you and the boys."

"Cloverville could suit you, too." If the fool would stop fighting those feelings for Colleen.

Nick shook his head.

"I heard you looked at the Barber place." Mrs. Applewhite had called. Apparently she was divorced, and looking for more than property.

"Small towns. Nothing goes unnoticed." Nick sighed, more resigned than disgusted. "I thought since there are no hotels, that it might be smart to have a place here. You know, for when the weather's bad."

"Okay."

Nick rubbed his hands over his face as if to remove paint, but Josh suspected it was mostly because he didn't dare meet his gaze. "Not that I'll need it," his friend went on. "I doubt I'll spend as much time in the office as you will."

"I heard you were already lining up appointments at the hardware store."

He laughed. "I didn't really have a choice. It was either that or Mr. Carpenter was going to take off his shirt so I could examine his shoulder. And Mrs. Hild…" Nick shook his head. "Their appointments aside, I'm really not going to be at the office much. I'll mostly be at the hospital, doing surgeries. Nothing has to change all that much."

"It already has," Josh spoke softly, the way he did to Buzz and TJ when they'd had a nightmare and he didn't want to scare them further. "*You've* changed."

Nick's face paled and he hotly denied it. "I haven't changed. We've just been here a week."

"It's been long enough for you to fall in love," Josh observed. Had he done the same thing—not with his bride but with her maid of honor?

"Don't make me hit you again," Nick threatened.

"You haven't taken a swing at me since I got drunk in college," Josh reminded him. "I had it coming, *then*." He'd gotten drunk and stupid over some girl he'd been seeing, when he'd caught her trying to kiss Nick.

"You do now, talking crazy." Nick shook his head. "I know you don't have much of a sense of humor, but this isn't funny, even for you."

"I'm not trying to be funny, but you know that," Josh pointed out. "I'm trying to have a serious discussion with my best friend, because I'm afraid he's going to throw away his one shot at true happiness."

"One shot. You think that's all we get?"

Josh laughed. "Not the rest of us. Only you. I've known you a long time, Nick, and you've never once let down your guard enough to fall in love."

"I didn't let down my guard." He bristled, probably feeling as if Josh had backed him into a corner. "I can't. She's just like Amy, like Molly, working at the hospital to catch a husband. I'm not fool enough to fall for that mantrap."

Josh laughed again, unoffended. "You're not as stupid as I am, huh?" Grinning, he shook his head. "You're an arrogant bastard."

"Hey!"

"And a gutless coward," Josh continued with the insults.

"You're really pushing me to hit you again," Nick threatened.

"Come on, Nick. You're grasping at any excuse, just because you're scared."

"I'm not husband material."

Josh laughed, with bitterness this time. "Apparently, neither am I."

"Come on. You believe in this crap."

"Crap?"

"Love." He snorted. "Happiness."

Josh's laugh grew heartier. "Only you would call love and happiness crap."

"Anything that fleeting can only be crap."

"Nick, it doesn't have to be fleeting," Josh persisted. Because he had a feeling if he let himself fall for Brenna Kelly, his love for her would last forever. That was why he couldn't fall, and why he'd been fighting his feelings. Why would he want to love a woman who'd no doubt leave him like every other woman he'd cared about—or thought he could care about—had?

Nick shrugged. "I haven't seen any proof that it lasts."

"My parents."

"Since that's the only example you've got, I'd call them a fluke. Look at all the people we work with, all the divorce horror stories we've heard."

"Our job. Our hours. It's hard on a relationship," Josh acknowledged. "That's why I wanted the private practice," he continued. "We can set our own hours. As few…"

"Or as many as we want," Nick agreed.

"You're already pulling double shifts."

"I didn't have scholarships—I've got loans to pay off. And now we have another one."

"You won't regret opening the office here," Josh assured him. Because he believed that eventually things would work out between Colleen and his best friend. He had less hope for himself.

Chapter Ten

Brenna stepped across the threshold that Josh had carried her over such a short time ago. With the hardwood floors gleaming and the walls painted the colors she'd chosen, the house had become the home she'd always known it could be.

Just not for her.

She followed the clink and clatter of noise into the kitchen. With the clever hands that had made his first wife beautiful, Dr. Towers turned a screwdriver on the hinge on one of the kitchen cabinets.

"You were right about the new hardware," he said, gesturing toward the black wrought-iron hinges and handles on the red oak. "You were right about the colors, too."

"It's done," Brenna said, taking in the sage-painted kitchen and family room.

"I almost feel guilty for outbidding you," Josh admitted.

"So let me have it," she teased him.

His blue eyes threw off sparks as he turned toward her. "I'd love to, but you're not interested."

"I'm interested in the *house*," she insisted. And him. But she shouldn't be. She couldn't be, not without losing herself and forsaking the loyalty to her friends that had always been such an integral part of who she was.

"I said almost," he reminded her. "I don't feel guilty enough to give it up."

"Where are your helpers?" she asked. His car had been the only one in the driveway. If she'd been stronger, she wouldn't have stopped but she'd been drawn irresistibly to the house...and to Josh.

"Rory pulled a muscle at his soccer game the other night, so he didn't come over," he explained.

"And Nick?"

He shrugged. "I think he got scared away."

"From Cloverville?" she asked.

"From Colleen."

She nodded. She'd thought something was going on between her young friend and the handsome doctor. "So he's scared of Colleen?"

"Of what he feels for her," Josh clarified.

Brenna could identify with the orthopedic surgeon's fear.

Josh sighed. "I just hope he doesn't blow his one shot at happiness."

"One shot?" she asked. "You think that's all a person gets?"

Josh nodded. Then he explained, "There's only one shot for a person like Nick, who's determined to fall for no one."

"And what about you?" she asked, her heart pounding as she waited for his answer. If he really believed all a person got was one shot, had the mother of his sons been his? Maybe loyalty to Molly wasn't the only reason Brenna had to fight her attraction to him.

"According to him, I fall too easily."

And maybe his best friend was right—Josh admitted to

himself but only to himself. He'd fallen fast for his first wife, although he'd realized after the fact that that had been more lust than love. And Molly... She was such a nice girl he'd been convinced he could fall for her. But instead he'd fallen for her maid of honor. He couldn't fight his feelings for Brenna any longer.

A week had passed. If Molly had changed her mind about marrying Josh, she would have been back before now. She would have at least called. Surely Brenna had to realize that her friend didn't want him. Did Brenna?

She didn't respond to Josh's comment, as if she wasn't interested in his love life—or his love. Instead she inspected the house, moving from room to room. Josh trailed every step she took in her high heels, watching her hips swaying in her khaki skirt. His head grew light. Probably from the paint fumes. Or maybe because all his blood had rushed to a lower part of his body.

"It's done," she said. "You can move in now."

And out of her house. Josh winced. He'd always known she wanted him gone, but still her rejection stung. "I couldn't have finished it without all your help."

She waved a hand, as if dismissing what she'd done. "I didn't do anything Molly wouldn't have done."

"I thought you weren't her second," he reminded her.

"No, I'm just her friend." Her husky voice, pitched even deeper, implied a warning.

Not to try anything with her again? "You've made that clear," he said.

"Not clear enough," she murmured.

"You've been a good friend to her," he insisted. "You went above and beyond the duties of the maid of honor for the wedding. And definitely for this house."

"It was bad enough losing the house to you," she said, her lips curving in a teasing smile. "I sure didn't want you messing it up."

He hadn't messed up the house, but he'd messed up everything else. If he hadn't proposed to Molly first, he might have had a shot with Brenna.

"Well, I appreciate how hard you worked," he said then teasingly added, "even though it was to get rid of me and the boys."

"I didn't want to get rid of the boys."

Josh forced a carefree grin. "Just me."

Brenna shook her head. "I wish I wanted to get rid of you."

Josh's breath caught. "You don't?"

Waves of red hair swirled around her bare shoulders. Today she wore a green silk tank top with the khaki skirt, looking both sophisticated and sexy.

"You are so beautiful," he said, reaching out to brush a lock of hair back from her face.

She arched an eyebrow and asked, "Did you smear paint on me again?"

"Who, me?" he asked, in mock innocence. When she continued to stare at him as hard as his old third-grade teacher used to, he buckled just as Mrs. Hoolihan had always made him buckle. Back then, he'd given up Nick as the one who'd shot spit wads into Sally Kruger's hair…even when it had been him. "Guilty."

"You don't always set a very good example for your sons," she admonished him.

Especially not with Nick, who was usually the brunt of Josh's practical jokes.

"You're lucky they're such good boys," she said.

He scrutinized her face to see if she was kidding. But

as Nick had been earlier, she was serious. "Yeah," he said, with pride, "they are."

"Despite you."

"Hey!" He laughed.

"No, you're a good father, Josh."

No compliment had ever meant as much to him. He stroked his fingers across her cheek. His throat thick with emotion, he rasped out a grateful, "Thank you."

Brenna stepped away from him, so that his hand dropped back by his side. And she blinked, as if breaking a connection between them. He wished it were that easy. Then she turned away, and clearing her throat she complimented the house, "It looks beautiful."

Not nearly as beautiful as she was.

"You really like this paint color?" he asked, gesturing toward the walls of the family room.

"I really like this house."

"I'm not giving up the house," Josh insisted as he stepped in front of her, so she'd have to look at *him* and not his house. "But I'd be willing to share it."

With Molly. Brenna reminded herself that he'd bought this house for her best friend. Not her. "You are sharing it," she reminded him, "with your sons."

"Thank you," he said, "for helping them to start thinking of this place as their home. I hope you'll come visit them." He touched her face again, his fingertips, rough from all the manual labor, stroking along her jaw to her cheek. "And me. Often."

Brenna bit her lip and nodded. "Sure. Of course."

He leaned closer, his mouth brushing her cheek where he'd streaked the paint that morning. "You are so beautiful."

Her pulse quickened with his touch, so she reminded

herself of his type. The woman in the magazine. Molly. "I'm no model." Nor had she ever wanted to be. "Like your first wife."

He pulled back slightly, and a muscle twitched along his jaw. "Nick told you?"

She shook her head. "No. The boys told me, when they showed me her picture in a magazine. One I guess you have already shown them."

"Were they okay when they saw her?" Josh asked, his eyes full of concern for his sons.

"They got a little emotional. That might have been because they were overly tired, though. I stopped by the bakery instead of bringing them right home to nap."

A faint smile stole across his mouth. "They really don't nap."

"No, they don't," she acknowledged with a sigh. "They talked Mama and Pop into taking them to the park again."

"They probably wanted to see the headless horseman." Josh shook his head as if awed by their imagination.

"They're talking about Colonel Clover," she explained. "The statue of our town founder."

"Well, I'm sure he's not headless."

"Actually, he is."

"What?" he asked with a deep laugh. "A headless statue? Maybe Nick's right about this town."

"He was the victim of a drive-by years ago," she explained. "Or a drive-through. I'm really not sure what to call it." An accident. And she wished her young friend would give herself a break over something that hadn't hurt anyone but Colleen herself.

"And here I thought Cloverville was a nice, safe place

to raise my kids," he teased. Yet concern for his sons still haunted his eyes.

She reached out and touched Josh's arm, running her fingers over the short, coarse hair. "But there are some things no father can protect his children from." Like the pain of their mother's abandonment.

He shook his head. "I wish I could have."

"So, the woman in the magazine…" The plastic-looking model. "She really is their mother?"

His shoulders jerked in a tense shrug. "Maybe I shouldn't have told them. But they ask about her, about why they don't have a mommy and everyone else in preschool does. They don't remember her, but they wanted to know what she looks like."

"She never visits?"

He shook his head.

"Never calls?"

He shook his head again.

"She just walked away from them?" Brenna asked, stunned. "And you?"

"Yes," he answered, with no perceptible trace of pain in his voice. Instead he focused on Brenna, running his fingers across her face to play with her hair.

"I don't understand."

"Maybe it's easier for her, and them, that she doesn't come back," Josh explained. "Maybe it's better to make a clean break."

Like Brenna needed to make with him. But temptation tingled along her skin with Josh's touch, as his fingers stroked her cheek, and then along her throat to her shoulder. "Josh…"

His eyes darkened with desire and something close to awe. "I've never met a woman like you."

She smiled. "Real?"

"Wonderful." His lips replaced his fingers as he kissed his way down her throat. Then, using his teeth, he pulled the strap of her tank top down her arm.

She shivered and lifted her hands, pushing her fingers into his thick, soft hair. She wanted to push him away, but she could only clutch him closer. She'd never wanted another man the way she wanted Josh Towers. If Molly was really committed to him, she would have been back before now. She would have been begging him to forgive her and take her back.

Brenna wanted to beg him to take her. "I…"

Josh pressed his mouth to hers, unwilling to hear her reiterate all the reasons they *shouldn't* be together. He wanted to show her that they *needed* to be together. He kissed her again and again, slipping his tongue between her lips.

She kissed him back with the same intensity of desire burning in his heart and throbbing in his tense body.

"Brenna…"

He slipped her straps down her shoulders, so that the green silk dropped to her waist. Then he pushed down the cups of her strapless bra and brushed his fingers over her breasts and the little cupcake tattoo. Still kissing her, he held the fullness of her heavy breasts and ran his thumb over the distended nipples. Back and forth, teasing her with his touch.

She arched her back and moaned against his mouth, then bit his lower lip. His hands smoothed down her sides to her hips and pulled her closer. She was so damned beautiful, so curvy and soft.

He fumbled with the clasp on her skirt. But Brenna's hands covered his, stopping him. Then she reached for the hem of his paint-spattered T-shirt and lifted it up. Her breath hissed out between her teeth as she pulled the shirt over his head. "You're the beautiful one, Josh."

Her hands skimmed over his chest, her fingers pushing through the dark hair. Then she leaned forward and pressed a kiss against his heart, which pulsed beneath her lips.

Too impatient to fumble with the clasp, he fisted his hands in the skirt and lifted the material. Then he lifted her onto the kitchen counter. He ran his hands over the warm, soft skin of her bare thighs, parting them and pushing aside her panties, so that he could make love to her with his mouth. She was so hot—so sweet.

Her nails bit into his shoulders and she screamed his name. "Josh!" Then her fingers gripped his hair, pulling him away. "We can't. Molly…"

Heart hammering hard, he reminded her, "She left me at the altar. She doesn't want me. And I don't want her. I want *you,* Brenna!" His body ached with wanting her.

The battle between guilt and desire waged in the depths of her green eyes. Just when Josh thought he'd lost she touched him, her nails skimming down his chest, over his stomach to the snap at the waistband of his jeans.

Air shuddered out of his lungs and he dared to breathe again. "Brenna…"

"I want you," she murmured, the rasp of her voice echoing in the rasp of his zipper as she undid his jeans.

Control snapping, Josh shucked his jeans and underwear, pausing only to retrieve a condom from his wallet. Brenna pulled the foil packet from his hand, ripped it open with her teeth and sheathed him, as impatient as he was. Pulling her closer to the edge of the counter, he pushed inside her. "You're so…"

She lifted her legs, wrapping them around his waist and taking him deeper. "It's been a while for me," she murmured, kissing his shoulder.

"Me, too…" But it had never felt like this with anyone else. Like coming home. He drove deeper yet, and she arched her back, taking all of him. "You're so hot."

Her nails gripped his shoulders again, and her body tensed. She came, shuddering and keening. "Josh…"

He thrust again, burying himself inside her. His legs shook with the intensity of the orgasm roaring through him. "Brenna!" His breathing harsh, he lowered his head, kissing first the top of her breast, then the little tattoo on the side. And now he lifted his mouth to hers. As he kissed her, he tasted salt. He pulled back, pulling out of her and lifted his hands to cup her face. Tears trailed down her cheeks.

"Oh, sweetheart…"

"We…" Her breath hitched. "We shouldn't have."

"Yes, yes, we should have," he insisted, feeling her slipping away even before she shoved him back.

Her eyes brimming with guilt and longing, she shook her head. "No. No…" Hands shaking, she pulled up the straps of her tank top. Then she wriggled off the counter and yanked down her skirt. "You're still Molly's."

Josh stood back, only watching as she ran away from him, like all the women before her. In her wake, he murmured, "I'm yours…"

But he'd screwed it up, like every relationship before her, because he'd rushed her. He pushed his hand through his sweat-damp hair, hating himself.

"I KNOW WE'RE SUPPOSED TO give her space, but I have to talk to her," Brenna insisted as she shoved open the door to Eric South's rustic log cabin and pushed past him. "Now!"

"She's not here," he said , closing the front door behind her.

He didn't follow her as she ran to each room of the small house, searching for Molly. When she walked back into the living room, Eric leaned against the door, his face stubbled with beard except for the scar on his left cheek. His gray eyes were dark with pain.

"She's gone." Brenna stated the obvious.

"Yeah."

The bleak tone of Eric's voice echoed Brenna's despair. She wasn't the only one hurting. She dropped her purse into one of the leather easy chairs. Obviously Eric needed a friend as much as she did.

"Do you have anything to drink?" she asked.

He straightened away from the door and crossed the small living room to the kitchen in the back of the house. The room consisted of vintage appliances, lacquered pine cabinets and counters. Brenna followed him and settled onto one of the stools pulled in front of the short breakfast bar.

"Iced tea? Lemonade?" Eric asked, his hand on the handle of the copper-coated fridge.

"I was thinking of something a little stronger," she admitted.

"I don't have any spiked punch," Eric said. A hint of humor lightened his smoky gray eyes.

"Spiked punch?" She narrowed her eyes. "Were you at the wedding?"

"There was no wedding," he reminded her.

"Nope. Because *your* friend skipped out before the ceremony. Why did she do that?" Brenna asked.

"*Your* friend," Eric said, "got cold feet."

The bleak note back in his deep voice had Brenna suspecting he wasn't talking about Josh any more. Had Molly gotten cold feet about *him*? About finally seeing Eric as more than just a friend?

"She's gone. Does that mean her feet warmed up?" Brenna asked as she glanced out the windows to where the sun set on the small fishing lake just outside Eric's patio doors.

Her old friend shrugged. "I don't know what she's going to do."

Her chest ached with regret at the thought of Molly returning to Josh. "Do you think she might want him back?"

"The *GQ* doc?" Instead of opening his fridge, Eric reached into the cupboard above it and extracted a dusty bottle of whiskey.

"*GQ* doc?" she repeated. "Is that what he's called around the hospital?" Eric, a paramedic, spent a lot of time at the hospital, too.

He nodded.

"So do you think she wants him back?"

He nodded again. "Why wouldn't she? He's got the looks. The money."

"The house," she interjected.

"Yeah, I heard he bought the Manning place," Eric admitted.

"You heard right." She stared him down. "I haven't seen you around at all this past week, yet you know everything that's been going on."

Half his mouth lifted in a grin. "I'm a Marine."

Ex-Marine, but Brenna noticed he never made that distinction. "You were a medic, not a spy," she reminded him.

"So, the Manning place… It's not the mini-mansion he

probably has in East Grand Rapids, but it's a pretty big house. What? Four, five bedrooms?" Eric remarked as he unscrewed the cap.

"Yeah." Brenna sighed. "He must want more kids, a bigger family."

"Molly would make a great mother." His hands shaking slightly, Eric grabbed two glasses from a cupboard and splashed some whiskey into them. Then he pushed one across the lacquered wood counter to Brenna.

She would make a great mother. Brenna wanted to be a mother, not just to provide her parents with the grandkids they wanted, but because she loved TJ and Buzz. She wanted to be *their* mother. She'd fallen as hard for them as she had their father.

"Do you think she loves him?" Brenna asked as guilt pushed down hard on her chest, making it tough for her to breathe as she waited for her friend's answer. No one, not even she, knew Molly the way Eric knew Molly.

He lifted his shoulders in a shrug so tense that it made him grimace. "I don't know what to think."

Brenna tapped her glass against his. "Cheers to that." She downed the fiery liquid in one cough-sputtering, tear-watering gulp.

"You're staying here, you know," Eric said as he sipped at his glass.

She didn't intend to have more than one drink, but she nodded. With the paint fumes in his new home, Josh wouldn't have been able to move in yet, and Brenna wasn't strong enough to be around him and his sons. She also suspected that Eric didn't want to be alone, either. Again.

She lifted her gaze to her long-time friend's face. Even with the scar, he was still damned good-looking—with those smoky eyes, his dark golden hair and muscular body. "Why did you and I never…" Then she nodded in response to her own question. "Molly."

He'd always loved Molly. What about Josh? Even though he claimed he didn't want her now, he must have wanted her enough to propose. Would he again, if she came back to him?

Chapter Eleven

Josh tugged up the zipper of his duffel bag, the last of his things packed. Making sure he hadn't overlooked anything, he glanced around the turret parlor. While he wouldn't miss the clutter and the lumpy foldout bed, he definitely would miss the Kellys' welcoming house. And Mama and Pop.

But most of all, he'd miss Brenna. Yet it was better this way. He'd screwed things up with her already, rushing her…right out the door. She hadn't even come home last night. Where had she stayed?

Knuckles wrapped softly against the French doors, and he released the breath he hadn't realized he'd been holding all night. She was home.

"Thank God you're back." But Brenna wasn't the woman standing in the doorway.

This woman, while curvy, was petite, with long, curly brown hair and wide brown eyes. Molly McClintock's lips curved into a slight smile. "Somehow I don't think you're talking about me."

"Molly…" Overwhelmed with guilt and disappointment, Josh closed his eyes. "Thank God you're all right."

"Yes." Her soft voice trembling with nerves, she said, "I know you probably hate me."

"No."

"You can't even *look* at me."

"That has nothing to do with what *you* did."

"Josh," she said, her tone light with amusement. "You didn't do anything wrong."

He opened his eyes and braced himself to confess. "You have no idea what's been going on since you left."

She smiled. "Oh, you'd be surprised what I know."

"I don't want to hurt you," he said, "I know when I proposed I made you a promise…"

"When I took off, *I* broke that promise," she interrupted him. "So anything you've done can't hurt me." Yet her dark eyes were sad, as if someone else had hurt her. Her smile returned, albeit forced. "So what have you done?"

"I think I'm falling for your best friend."

"Eric?" she teased.

"Brenna…"

"Good." Her dark eyes gleamed then with satisfaction and triumph.

"What?" He pushed a hand through his hair. "You wanted me to fall for someone else?"

She shook her head. "Just Brenna. I realized a while ago that you two were perfect for each other. And I should have broken our engagement then. But I was being selfish."

Because she loved him and hadn't wanted to let him go? "Molly, I'm sorry…"

"I'm the one who should be sorry," she insisted. "I don't love you. I never should have accepted your proposal in the first place."

Josh shook his head. "I don't understand…"

"Neither do I and that's why I took off. I needed to sort out some things." She tapped a fingertip against her temple.

"So, have you?"

She nodded, and pain flickered through her eyes. "For all the good it's done me. I really made a mess of things."

Josh sighed. "You're not the only one." He pushed a slightly shaking hand through his hair. "I don't even know where Brenna is."

"I think she's with Eric," Molly said, her voice soft with sympathy. "At least I saw her car parked by his cabin."

A laugh bubbled out of the pressure on his chest. "So I've lost two women to this man I've never met."

"I think we both know that you never had me. And I never had you. We're just friends, Josh," she said, crossing the room to his side. Always warm and generous, she took his hand in hers and squeezed. "That's not enough. We both need, we both *deserve* more."

"I know." Although he wasn't sure he deserved her, he certainly wanted Brenna.

Molly released his hand, leaving something cold and metallic within his palm—her engagement ring. As he shoved it into his pocket, she wistfully mused, "I guess some friends are just friends."

"Is that true of you and Eric South?"

Now tears brightened her eyes. "I'm not sure we're even friends anymore."

Josh pulled her into a hug, loving her as he would a little sister—a friend. Not as he loved Brenna. Did *she* even consider them friends any more? Somehow he doubted it.

"DID JOSH FORGET SOMETHING?" Pop asked as he slapped a hand onto her shoulder.

Brenna shook her head. But she couldn't turn. She couldn't face her father. "Are Buzz and TJ all settled into their new house?"

"I think so." Her dad sighed. "I'm going to miss those little guys."

The sadness in her father's voice had her turning to comfort him. "Josh will let you see them whenever you want."

"I know," Pop agreed, his green eyes clouding wistfully, "I'm sure he'll even let us take them overnight from time to time."

"Sure he will." God, she had to find another house soon. She didn't want to avoid the boys, but she had to avoid Josh or she'd let herself fall even deeper and more hopelessly in love with him.

"Of course," Pop assured himself with a grin. "Josh is a great guy. Wonderful father. And every dang woman in town is gaga over him. That busybody Mrs. Hild along with Mrs. Carpenter kept looking for excuses to stop by when we were working on the house." He chuckled and shook his head.

"Cloverville has really welcomed him," Brenna acknowledged. But no one else had welcomed him as she had. How could she have betrayed Molly like that? How could she have betrayed herself?

"I thought you did, too," her father said, with a bit of censure.

"I did."

"But then you didn't come home last night. He was worried about you."

Remorse tugged at her. "Just *him*?"

"Mama and I know you can take care of yourself," he said, then sighed. "Too well."

"What do you mean?"

"Well, you take care of yourself so well that you don't seem to need anyone else."

Brenna wrapped her arms around her father's ample girth and squeezed. "I'll always need you and Mama," she assured him.

Pop laughed and cupped her head, petting her hair as if she were a cat. "Oh, honey, you haven't needed us for a long while, but I don't know what we'd do without you."

Heat rushed to her face. "Pop, you know I can't stay your little girl forever," she said, deciding to finally broach the subject of her moving out. "I've already started looking for a place of my own."

"Mama and I had hoped you'd found it," he said.

His words stunned her. "What?" She'd expected resistance to her desire to move out—that was why she hadn't mentioned her plans yet.

"With Josh and Buzz and TJ. That's your place, honey," he said.

Brenna fought the urge to bury her face in her father's shoulder and weep. "That's not my place, Pop. That's Molly's."

"If Molly wanted him, she would have married him," her father insisted.

"She got cold feet. She'll figure out what she gave up." And then she'd want him back. Brenna decided it would have been better to have never had him than to have to give him up. Despite what they'd done in his kitchen, though, she'd never *really* had him.

Pop shook his head. "Molly's a smart girl. She knows where she belongs. It's not with Josh. *You* belong with Josh."

Blinking back tears, Brenna smiled. "You just want those twins for your grandkids," she teasingly accused him.

"I love those boys. And with two, Mama and I don't have to fight over them," Pop agreed with a wide grin.

"I knew…"

"But Mama and I just want you to be happy," he insisted. "You deserve it, girl."

"I deserve a man who loves me," she pointed out. "For me." And not as a substitute for another woman.

"Yes, you do," her father agreed.

"Someone's here to see you," Mama called up from the foyer.

Hope flitted through Brenna. Had Josh come back—for her? She turned for the stairs and just barely resisted the urge to descend them at a run. She expected to see Josh with flowers and another apology for Mr. Hyde's behavior.

But no man stood next to Mama, just a familiar woman with curly brown hair and a tentative smile.

"Hi, Brenna." While Molly McClintock greeted her as casually as if they were meeting to go to a movie, her expressive eyes were dark with guilt and regret.

"Molly." The disappointment at her guest not being Josh drained away, leaving only relief that her friend was all right. She flung her arms around the smaller woman, pulling her into as tight an embrace as a mother would her missing child. "Thank God, you're all right."

"Of course I'm all right," Molly said, but when Brenna pulled back she noted that sadness dimmed the usual brightness of her friend's smile.

"I've been worried about you," Brenna said.

"We all have," Mama added as she patted Molly's back. "I'll leave you two girls alone to catch up."

Brenna smiled at her mother's comment, as if they were still teenagers brimming with gossip and drama. *If they'd known then what they knew now…*

Of course Molly's teenage life had been truly dramatic. She'd lost her father. Then her true best friend, Eric, had left for the Marines, even though Molly had begged him not to. She hadn't wanted to lose him, too. She hadn't lost him then, but Brenna wondered if Molly had lost him now. He'd been pretty upset the other night.

"Eric's been worried about you, too," she shared with Molly, following the beauty as the other woman stepped back out onto the porch.

"Eric?" Molly's big eyes widened even more. "But I was with him…"

"I know," Brenna said. "I think everyone," even Josh, "knew where you were. But he said you left his place a couple of days ago. Eric's pretty broken up about it."

"That's his fault," Molly said, her usually soft voice sharp with bitterness and anger. "I'm done blaming myself for *everything*."

"Molly…"

"I'm sorry about the wedding," she said, "about all your hard work for nothing. I feel so bad about that, but I couldn't marry Josh."

Finally, Brenna asked the question that was burning in her mind since Molly's brother Clayton had walked into the back of the church without the bride. "Why not?"

Molly shook her head, as if disgusted with herself. "I couldn't marry a man I didn't love and who didn't love me."

Brenna had suspected, even before Molly had gone out

the church window, that her friend hadn't loved her fiancé. Mostly because she'd always thought Molly loved another man, Eric. "I don't understand why any woman, let alone a smart woman like you, would agree to marry a man she didn't love?"

"A selfish woman would," Molly admitted. "A scared woman. After what my mom went through losing my dad, I honestly didn't want to marry a man I loved. Because if I lost him, I was scared I wouldn't survive…"

"Oh, Molly…" Brenna wrapped her arm around her friend's slight shoulders. "I understand your being scared." And she didn't know what to say to offer comfort. It did hurt like hell losing someone you loved, even if you'd never really had him. "But you're not selfish."

Molly sniffled and nodded. "Yes, I am. I wasn't being fair to Josh. Look at him. What woman wouldn't be able to fall in love with him?"

God knew Brenna had tried not to, but she hadn't been able to resist him. She pulled away from her friend and stammered, "I…"

"I remember how awed I was the first time I met him," Molly said with a wistful sigh.

Jealousy stung Brenna. "He is good-looking."

"Yes, he is," Molly agreed as she leaned against the porch railing. "But that wasn't what awed me. He's so much more than his looks."

She didn't have to tell Brenna, who intimately knew how much more Josh was—a lover, a friend and a wonderful, loving father.

Molly continued, "He works in this field that has so much pain, so much ugliness, and he turns it into something beautiful. He's truly gifted."

"Are you sure you don't love him?" Brenna asked.

Molly smiled. "Nope. But I respect him. And I think we're still friends. I talked to him this morning as he was packing up his stuff."

"Yes, he was staying here," Brenna admitted, "while he worked on the Manning house. Did you know he bought it?" For Molly.

"Colleen told me," Molly said. "I'm not surprised he bought a house here. The first moment he saw Cloverville, he fell for the town."

"He wants what's best for Buzz and TJ," Brenna explained.

"Thanks for taking care of him and the boys," Molly said. "You're such a wonderful friend."

Brenna's face heated under her friend's penetrating gaze. "I, uh…"

"And because Josh is my friend, too, I want the best for him. I want him to find a woman who truly loves him and only him."

Brenna's face heated even more. She lifted her palms to her hot skin. "But what if he loves you, Molly?" He'd claimed he didn't, but had that been just his hurt feelings talking?

"He probably does love me," Molly admitted.

Brenna sucked in a breath, as if someone had stabbed her. "Of course."

"But only as a friend," Molly added. "I've had hotter kisses from Pop."

"I know why you agreed to a loveless marriage. But if you're right about Josh not loving you, why would he propose?" She suspected Molly hadn't been the only selfish one in that relationship. "Was he just looking for a mother for Buzz and TJ?"

Molly sighed. "He never lied to me. He never claimed

to love me, but he cares about me. He thought it would be enough. Things were comfortable between us without the messy emotions of falling in love."

Brenna could relate to wanting to avoid the pain she felt now, since her heart was heavy with it. "So why did you change your mind about marrying him?" she had to know. "If you're determined to *not* marry someone you love?"

"I changed my mind about that, too." Molly sighed. "I want the mess."

"Me, too," Brenna admitted.

"Then go after Josh," Molly urged her. "You have my blessing."

"I, uh…"

Molly grinned. "You've already gotten involved with him."

Tears stung Brenna's eyes. "I'm sorry I was such a horrible friend. I should have waited to make sure you didn't love him, that you didn't want him back."

Molly pulled her into a quick hug. "Hush. I was the horrible friend, letting you do all the work for the wedding, then skipping out. I was so ashamed and so sorry. I called a few times."

"You called?"

"I talked to Mama and Pop, but they said you were out. And I didn't have the guts to call your cell. I didn't know what to say to you, how to apologize."

"Don't worry about it," Brenna assured her friend. "Everything's fine." Between the two of them. She wasn't sure why her parents hadn't relayed the message that Molly had called. Obviously Molly's mother wasn't the only matchmaker in town.

Molly shook her head and wiped away Brenna's tears.

"It's not fine. You wouldn't be this unhappy if everything was fine."

"It's messy," Brenna admitted.

"I can tell that you already love him," Molly said. "Does he love you?"

Brenna shook her head. "Why would he love me?"

"Because you're perfect for him and Buzz and TJ."

"I'm far from perfect," Brenna said with a shaky laugh at her friend's blind loyalty. "Or I wouldn't have betrayed our friendship."

"You didn't betray anything," Molly assured her. "I admit to a little meddling myself. I'd like to see you and Josh together—happy."

But Brenna wasn't sure she could be happy with Josh. Would being with a plastic surgeon bring back all those old insecurities that she'd conquered long ago? Would she go back to feeling like the fat girl who wasn't as beautiful as her thinner friends?

"What about you, Molly? What about your happiness?" Brenna asked. "Do you want me to push someone down and sit on him for you?"

"If I thought it would help…" Molly smiled albeit with tears sparkling in her eyes. "I guess the old adage is true."

"Which one?"

"Be careful what you wish for," Molly warned. "I didn't want to marry a man I loved. Now I don't have that option."

"I don't understand…" Was Molly talking about Eric or someone else?

But she had a feeling the adage applied to Brenna as well as Molly. She'd wanted Josh, when she hadn't thought she could have him. But now, now she was scared that if she got what she wanted, she'd lose more of herself than she'd gain.

Chapter Twelve

TJ squirmed beneath the blankets Josh pulled up to his chin. Maybe fire engine red hadn't been such a good choice for his bedroom walls. Although the child had insisted red was his favorite color, it wasn't exactly restful.

Buzz, in the bottom bunk, tugged at Josh's pant leg. "Daddy?"

While each had their own bedroom, they took turns sleeping in each other's, unwilling yet to separate from each other. "Yes, Buzz?"

"I miss Mama and Pop," the little boy whined.

"And Brenna," TJ added.

They were unwilling to separate from the Kellys, too. Josh sighed. They weren't the only ones. "I thought you guys liked our new house now."

"Yeah, it doesn't stink now. So I like it," Buzz admitted.

"Why can't Pop and Mama come live with us?" TJ asked.

"They have their own house." Josh repeated his old argument, the one he'd been having with the boys since they'd moved out of the Kellys' and into their own place.

"What about Brenna? Can't she come live with us?" Buzz asked.

"No. Brenna lives with Mama and Pop."

"I wish she lived with us," Buzz pouted.

"Mama and Pop are going to take you to the Binder Park zoo tomorrow," Josh reminded them. He sure hoped the older Kellys knew what they were getting into—even an hour-long drive with the twins was a challenge.

"You're going to be good for them," he warned them with his sternest look.

They giggled. So he took turns tickling each squirming belly, giving them something to giggle about.

"You and Brenna come with us," Buzz said, between gasps for breath.

"Yeah!" TJ shouted his agreement.

"No, I have to check on the office. And I'm sure Brenna's working tomorrow."

Buzz's bottom lip protruded again, and TJ flopped over on his side, to face the wall, away from his father. All he did was disappoint them.

"You'll have fun with Mama and Pop," he assured them as he kissed each good-night. "Sleep tight. Don't let the bed bugs bite."

Neither of them chuckled, the way they usually did at their good-night ritual. Josh turned on TJ's fire engine nightlight before shutting off the overhead fixture. Drawing the door to within a foot of being closed, he stepped into the hall. His twins weren't the only ones disappointed that they didn't see more of Brenna.

The soft slam of a closing door drew his attention to the living room and lifted his heart with hope. *Brenna*?

"You've haven't even lived here two weeks yet and already you're leaving your doors unlocked," Nick scoffed, shaking his head with disgust as he walked into the living room.

"What brings you back to Cloverville already?" Josh asked. "The office isn't done yet." Not even with his checking on it every day for want of something better to do than think about what he might have had with Brenna.

Color tinged the other doctor's face. "I have a question to ask you."

"Well, this time you'll get the answer you want to hear," Josh assured him. "I talked to Molly—a few days ago, actually."

Nick nodded. "I know. Colleen said she was back."

"Colleen?"

Nick's mouth lifted in the biggest grin Josh had ever seen on his friend's face. "Don't play innocent with me. Colleen got the keys for my condo from you."

Josh shuddered in mock fear. "I didn't dare *not* give her the keys. I figured you deserved whatever she was going to dish out."

Nick sighed. "I don't think I deserve her. Not yet. But I'm going to spend the rest of my life trying."

"Nick?" he checked. "Is it really you? Can this lovesick fool really be my cynical friend?"

Nick laughed. "I deserve that. Except that I was the fool when I said that..."

"That love is crap?" Josh reminded him.

"Yeah. So go ahead. Say it. *I told you so,*" Nick urged him. "You've earned the right."

"It's ironic really. I realized a while ago that *you* were right, about my rushing into relationships." That was why he hadn't gone back to the Kellys' house or stopped by the bakery to see Brenna. And that was why he forced himself to stay away from her even though he ached to see her, to touch her...

He cleared his throat. "Now look at you, falling for Colleen McClintock less than two weeks after finally noticing her."

"It didn't even take a week," Nick corrected him. "That first time I saw her at the church, I fell, and I fell hard."

"Like I always knew you would when you met the right woman."

"Like you fell for Brenna Kelly."

Josh didn't bother lying to his friend. "You're right. I guess I am crazy. Even before I was *officially* unengaged I was falling for someone else. Talk about rushing things."

"When it's right, it's right," Nick insisted. "And I've seen you and Brenna together, and you're *right*."

"It's too soon," Josh argued.

Nick shook his head. "I wish I'd asked Colleen to marry me that first moment I knew, instead of wasting all this time fighting my feelings. You and I—we're surgeons—we know how precious and how finite time is. Don't waste it, Josh. You love Brenna. So tell her."

Josh dropped onto the edge of his new leather sofa, too stunned to stand. "You *what*? What did you do?"

Grinning like an idiot, Nick admitted, "I asked Colleen to marry me."

"And she didn't run screaming for the hills?" he teased, knowing his friend wouldn't be grinning like a fool if she had. He would be running after her.

Nick's eyes shined with love and pride. "No, she said yes."

Josh stood up and shook Nick's hand then slapped his back as they shared a brief, manly hug. "Congratulations, man."

"I just have one more question to ask you," Nick said.

Smothering a sigh in anticipation of another Jameson lecture, Josh nodded. "Ask away."

"Will you be my best man?"

"Of course. I got your back."

"Always," Nick agreed. "And I've got yours. So listen to me for once. Don't waste any more time. Go after Brenna."

Josh nodded, knowing that as always his friend was right. But he didn't trust himself to not mess things up again. He needed help.

THE WALLS SHOOK and the windows rattled as the door slammed. This time Josh had no doubt that his visitor was Brenna Kelly.

"Hey, don't hurt the house," he teased as she stalked into the living room, her high heels pounding into the polished hardwood. "You helped fix this place…"

"And that's why you should have told me you're getting rid of it!" she accused him, her face flushed nearly as red as her wavy hair.

"I'm not getting rid of it," he assured her. He thought about feeding her the "you're beautiful when you're angry" line, since it was certainly relevant. But having never seen her temper before, he decided not to push his luck. For now it was enough that she was here. *God, he'd missed her…*

She must have come directly from her office, as with the high-heeled sandals she wore a dress—in a yellow and tan pattern—that wrapped around her curves and tied at her waist. To get her out of it, did he need only untie that one knot? His fingers twitched with the temptation to find out.

"Josh!" she called his name, drawing his attention back to her face. Anger hardened her green eyes. "Pop told me you put the house up for sale."

"Pop lied."

Her voice shook as she insisted, "My father has *never* lied to me."

"He did. Just this time," he explained. "Because I asked him to."

"My father lied to me—for you?" she repeated, shaking her head as if stunned.

"I'm sorry."

"No, you're not," she called him on his lie. "You set this all up…" She gestured around the living room—at the candles flickering from every surface—and she shook her head. "And I bet Mama and Pop are keeping the boys overnight on this *zoo* trip."

"That's a long trip for the boys and your parents to make twice in one day."

"That's true," she allowed, "probably the only thing that's true. So what else do you have planned?"

The rest of their lives, if she'd agree. "I want to talk."

"Could have fooled me," she said. "You haven't called since you moved out."

"I didn't think you'd want to hear from me."

Her anger evaporated to leave only hurt. She'd wanted to hear from him—too much. "Why?"

"I'd rushed you into something you weren't ready for." He pushed a hand, which trembled slightly, through his thick, dark hair. "You didn't want to betray your friendship, but I kept pushing…"

"I talked to Molly."

He nodded. "Me, too. She gave me back the engagement ring. We're officially over."

"For almost a week now," she pointed out. "But you still didn't call me. You didn't even call me today. You *tricked* me into coming to see you."

"I'm sorry," he said. "I should have called."

She shook her head, hating that she felt small—petty. That he made her feel that way. "No. Like Molly, you were entitled to time alone, to figure out what you really want."

"I didn't need time."

Brenna's breath caught as he stepped closer to her and his hands cupped her shoulders.

"I know I want *you.*" His fingers skimmed up and down her arms. "It's been killing me to stay away from you this past week. But I wanted to give you time to figure out what you want."

She wanted *him. Be careful what you wish for…*

His hands cupped her face, his thumbs stroking the edge of her jaw. "I've missed you so much…"

Brenna lifted her hands to his shoulders, then slid them around to the back of his neck, pulling his head down until his mouth touched hers.

He deepened the kiss, his tongue sliding between her lips, in and out of her mouth. His hands slid down her back to her hips, pulling her closer to the hard length of his tense body. "I missed you so damn much," he murmured against her mouth.

"I missed you, too," she admitted, tears stinging her eyes. "And Buzz and TJ." Staying away, after spending so much time with him and them, had been torture.

He tortured her now with his touch, his hands sliding over her hips to her waist, his fingers plucking at the knot that held her dress closed.

"I thought you wanted to talk," she reminded him, her pulse quickening.

"We can talk later," he murmured against her neck, as his lips slid down her throat, nibbling and kissing.

Even though his breath warmed her skin, Brenna shivered. "Yeah, we can talk later…"

His hands slid back over her hips, but instead of pulling her closer, he set her away from him. His voice hoarse, he said, "Let me show you the house now."

Frustration formed a knot in her belly. "I don't want to see the house now," she protested, reaching for him again. In faded jeans and a navy-blue T-shirt, he was as ridiculously handsome as he'd been a tux. As ridiculously irresistible…

He caught her hand in his, tugging her toward the hall. Brenna stumbled after him, still protesting, "I've already seen the house."

"Not since I got the furniture moved in here," he argued.

"Nice stuff," she commented, barely remembering the leather couch and mahogany coffee tables in the living room as he led her down the hall.

"What about this?" he asked, opening a door, then stepping back for her to enter. "What do you think of my bed?"

Brenna's frustration eased, replaced with a quiver of anticipation. She passed in front of him, her heels sinking into the plush carpeting. He'd lit candles in this room, too, and the flickering flames reflected off the walls. She hadn't chosen the color in here—she hadn't considered the master bedroom her place. So he'd picked, a red so deep the walls looked like velvet.

"It's beautiful," she said, awed.

"You can't tell how great a bed is by looking at it," he argued. "You have to test it out."

Brenna turned back to him. The candlelight reflected in his eyes, as if he were burning—with desire for her. Fighting to keep a smile from her lips, she shook her head. "I don't need to test it out," she teased.

He closed the distance between them with long, deter-mined strides. "You're testing *me*," he threatened, reaching for her.

Brenna stepped back until her legs hit the edge of the mattress, the satin comforter brushing against her bare skin. "Josh…"

As he trapped her between his body and the bed, a grin lifted the corners of his mouth and brightened his eyes. "Now I have you right where I want you." Yet he shook his head. "But you're overdressed." He touched her then. Just his fingers at her waist, he tugged loose the knot of her dress.

Excitement quickened Brenna's pulse so it pounded madly in her throat. She loved Josh like this, lighthearted, teasing…

She loved Josh.

He pushed the dress from her shoulders so that she stood before him naked but for a thin slip and her lacy bra. He groaned. "You are so damned gorgeous…"

"You just want to get me into your bed," she accused him, smiling.

"Yes, I do."

"I don't want to try it out alone," she insisted, reaching for the hem of his T-shirt. She dragged the navy cotton over his head, ruffling his thick, dark hair. The T-shirt dropped to the floor at the same moment he dropped his jeans, leaving him in nothing but boxers and a wide grin. His shoulders were so broad. His chest, beneath soft, black hair, was so muscular. He was perfect. Too perfect. "Josh…"

He dipped his head, kissing first her mouth, then her bare shoulder. His breathing harsh, he beseeched her, "Let me make love to you, Brenna."

She shook her head. "No." When he opened his mouth to protest, she pressed her palm over his lips, then with her free hand, she hooked her index finger in the waistband of his boxers. His erection throbbed, the moist tip touching her finger. "Make love *with* me."

"Yes, yes…" He fumbled with the clasp of her bra, dropping the garment to the floor atop her dress. Then he pushed down her slip, his palms gliding over her hips. His fingers stroked under the elastic of her panties, teasing her with fleeting touches.

She trembled, her knees weakening. She clutched at him, her nails digging into his shoulders. Then she skimmed her hands over his chest, the soft hair tickling her palms. This time, when she grabbed the waistband of his boxers, she pushed them down. His erection sprang free, nudging her hip.

"I want to take my time with you," he warned her as she reached for him, closing her hand around the hard length of him. "I want to love every inch of you." So he pushed her down onto the bed.

The feather-soft mattress cradled her, and the satin comforter was smooth and cool against her bare back. "Josh…"

He followed her down, his chest pressing lightly against her breasts as he balanced his upper body weight on the palms braced next to her head. His mouth slid from her throat, along her shoulder to the curve of her breast. "You are so beautiful."

"Josh…" She wrapped her arms around his back, pulling him all the way down onto her. Needing him close.

"I'm too heavy," he protested.

"Don't worry," she assured him, "I'm not going to break." Not her body. But maybe her heart. Could she trust him with it?

Josh's control snapped as he realized Brenna spoke the

truth. He didn't have to reign in his passion with her. Of all the women he'd ever known, she could handle it. She could handle him.

He kissed her again, with all the passion he felt for her. Despite her arms holding him close, he eased back and skimmed his hands down her body, stroking soft, alabaster skin.

He cupped her breasts, but they overflowed his hands, heavy and full, the nipples distended, begging for his touch. He rolled each hard tip between his thumb and forefinger.

A moan slipped from Brenna's lips and she moved her head against the sheets, arching her body toward his. "Josh…"

He bent his head and touched just the tip of his tongue to her nipple. She jumped as if he'd shocked her. But he'd done nothing yet—nothing compared to what he intended to do to her. He pulled the nipple into his mouth, nipping it with his teeth, laving it with his tongue while he traced the cupcake tattoo with his fingertip.

"Josh…" She parted her legs so that she cradled his hips, his erection pushing against her soft belly. She arched, rubbing against him.

He groaned, pulling her nipple deeper into his mouth, while his fingers smoothed over the warmth and fullness of her other breast. He teased that nipple with his thumb, flicking it back and forth over the hard point.

Brenna's body trembled beneath his as if she fought the sexual frustration that was obviously building inside her. "Josh…"

He eased back and skimmed his other hand down, between their bodies, beneath the flimsy elastic of her underwear. He pushed his fingers through curls to stroke her heat, to plunge inside her.

She tensed and shuddered, screaming his name, "Josh!"

He lifted his fingers to his mouth, tasting her passion, wanting more. He backed off the mattress to kneel next to the bed. Then he tore off her thin panties and made love to her with his mouth. *She was so damned sweet...*

Brenna's world shattered as she came. She unclenched her fingers from the satin spread, then willed some strength back into her muscles. And she reached for him, pulling him onto the mattress with her. She kissed his throat where his pulse hammered. Then she kissed her way down his chest, flicking her fingers across his nipples.

"Brenna..." His eyes filled with passion.

She wanted to give him more. So much more. She lowered her head, her lips trailing across the rippling muscles of his washboard abs. She dipped her tongue into his navel, but his erection nudged her cheek, throbbing with a demand for attention.

She wanted only to give him the pleasure he'd given her. First she closed her hand around him, stroking up and down the impressive length of him. He groaned and a cord strained in his neck. Then she leaned over and closed her lips around him, her breasts bumping against his hard thighs.

Like her fingers in the satin, Josh's tangled in her hair, holding her to him before pulling her away. "No, Brenna..."

"But I want..."

He pulled her up, into his arms and kissed her. "I want you. I want to bury myself deep inside you." He groaned again.

"Do it," she urged. She parted her legs. "Make love to me, Josh."

Josh's control, whatever he'd managed to hang on to

during her sensual assault on his body, snapped. He lifted one of her legs, rubbing her inner thigh against his hip. Then he drove deep into her wet heat.

Her muscles clutched him, and as she arched her hips, pulled him deeper yet until he was buried inside her—until he became part of her. He had never felt as connected to another person. "Brenna…"

He wanted to profess his love, tell her everything in his heart. But words escaped him. So, his body shuddering and begging for release, he could only show her. He withdrew, then entered again, thrusting in and pulling out.

Brenna's nails bit into his shoulders, then skimmed down his back as she pulled him closer. Her breasts pushed against his chest. He rubbed against her nipples, teasing her.

She reached up, nipping at the cords in his throat with her teeth. Then she pressed her mouth against his skin. Her body tensed, then melted and poured over him. "Josh! Josh! Josh!" She shouted her release.

He clenched the muscles in his stomach, his jaw, trying to hold back his own desperate need to seek release. He moved slowly, teasing her until she came again, tears streaking from the corners of her eyes to dampen her gorgeous red hair.

"Josh!" She murmured his name, her eyes wide with shock as if she were amazed by what she felt, the pleasure he had given her.

He hoped he glimpsed something more in her eyes. He hoped he saw love. Because he certainly felt it.

She arched against him, skimming her nails beyond his back to clutch his butt, so he thrust deeper. Unable to restrain himself any longer, he came, his body erupting with passion and desire. He came and he came, and he fell even deeper in love with this woman.

BRENNA STRETCHED and rolled over, reaching across the bed for Josh. But her hand skimmed across cold, tangled sheets. She blinked open her eyes to the sun streaming through the wood blinds, illuminating every corner of the master bedroom. Where had he gone?

"Hey, sleepyhead," a deep voice said as Josh walked into the bedroom. Muscles straining in his bare arms, he balanced a breakfast tray. A vase of roses, red like the paint on the walls, teetered as he set the tray across her lap, so she caught the flowers, and a thorn snagged her finger. He caught her hand and kissed the bleeding digit. "That's not exactly what I had in mind when I stole the roses from Mrs. Hild's yard. I didn't want to hurt you."

Here it came. The kiss-off.

"I'm a big girl," she assured him. Even with him and Molly officially over, Brenna had known she had no future with him. She wasn't his usual type. "I knew what I was getting into."

"Did you?" he asked as he dropped onto the bed next to her. He wore only his boxers, his chest bare and incredibly sexy. His hair mussed and his eyes shining with...love? Dare she hope?

"You snuck into Mrs. Hild's yard like that?" she couldn't stop herself from asking.

He shrugged. "It was dark yet." Only the first light of morning glinted through the windows.

No wonder Mrs. Hild hadn't shot him, as she'd threatened some other town miscreants, for stealing her beloved flowers. Never having had children of her own before her husband had died, the old woman had made her garden her baby.

"You know they're a handful," he said.

"What?" She narrowed her eyes, confused by his conversation and trying to understand exactly what he was saying to her.

"My boys," he elaborated. "They're a handful. But you know that."

"They're wonderful." And so was he. She had never had as considerate and thorough a lover. Her body ached, from what they'd done and from wanting more despite their having made love most of the previous day and night.

The pressure on her chest eased, as she realized he wasn't dumping her. Yet could they have a future together?

"They think you're wonderful. They love you already." He grinned. "Buzz and TJ are going to be so happy."

"What are we going to tell them?" she asked, wondering how a parent explained his relationship to his kids. Would she stay a friend or had she earned the title of girlfriend?

His grin widened, and his eyes sparkled. "We're going to tell them that we're finally going to have that wedding."

"What?" Her body jerked with shock, and she nearly toppled over the tray. A ring rolled across the wooden surface. They'd only known each other—really known each other—for two weeks, and he was proposing? Was he that desperate for a wife that he would propose to the next woman he met after Molly dumped him?

"And now you've spoiled the surprise." He laughed, appearing as excited as his boys had when they'd found the colonel's head in the park. "Hell, I guess *I* spoiled the surprise."

"Surprise?" She shouldn't have been shocked. She'd known he'd proposed almost as quickly to Molly.

He picked up the ring from the tray and reached for her hand. "This is only temporary," he said. "I figured you'd want to pick out your own engagement ring."

"Whose ring is this?" Her stomach lurched over the possibilities. "Molly's? Amy's?"

The grin slid away from his face. "No. It's mine. My parents gave it to me when I graduated med school."

"Your ring?" She turned her attention to the ring. The platinum-and-onyx band was definitely not an engagement ring.

"I don't wear it much because of surgeries and such. But it means a lot to me. It's proof of what I can accomplish with a lot of hard work."

Was that what he considered her? Hard work? Would he want to change her, like he'd changed Amy? Numb with shock, she let him slide the ring onto her finger. The platinum band wobbled around her knuckle—it was too big. Like she was for him. Too big. Too much. Too real.

Because she wanted a real marriage. Real love. Not the marriage of convenience he'd proposed to Molly. "It doesn't fit."

"It's only temporary. Until we find you the ring you want," he said. "We can make a trip to Grand Rapids, to the jewelers, and you can pick out any ring you want."

Maybe she could. But she couldn't have it. Fingers trembling, she pulled off his ring and set it back on the tray alongside the vase and a plate of toasted homemade bread slathered with melting butter and jam. Her stomach churned again, as queasy as if she'd let Buzz and TJ spin her on the merry-go-round in the park. Her usually healthy appetite gone. "No, I don't want a ring."

"You just want a wedding band?"

She blinked back the tears blurring her vision of the ring as she stared at the tray he'd brought her. And she lied. It was easier than telling him the truth—less painful. "I don't want a wedding."

"What? I thought you loved me?"

She had never said the words, but apparently he'd learned her secret. She couldn't deny her feelings. "I do," she admitted. "I love you."

"And I love you," he said as he reached for her.

She pressed her palms against his chest, holding him back. "Nick was right."

"What?" His brow furrowed with confusion. "What the hell does Nick have to do with this?"

"He said you fall in love too easily," she reminded him. "He was right."

"I fought falling for you, Brenna," he said, his voice ringing with sincerity. "I didn't want to make another mistake."

She believed him. "But you did. You made a mistake thinking I'd fill in for Molly." To be her second, her substitute.

"Molly?" he asked, as if perplexed. "What does she have to do with us?"

"Two weeks ago you were going to marry her," she reminded him. "My best friend."

"I didn't love her."

"But you were there—in the church. *You* didn't go out the window. You were standing by the altar waiting for her. If she had walked down that aisle, you would have married her." She swallowed hard. "You didn't love her, and you don't really love me." Her voice hoarse, she accused him, "You're just looking for a mother for your boys."

"Brenna!"

Not that she didn't want to be their mother. She loved

them. She loved Josh. But if she settled for companionship and chemistry, she was setting a bad example for them and cheating herself.

"I love you, Brenna."

She shook her head. "I thought I could get over the fact that you'd been about to marry my friend. And I probably could have, if we took this relationship slow and just dated, but that's not what you want. You want marriage. *Only* marriage."

"I want you. Only you!"

"Nope." She shook her head, letting loose one tear from her brimming eyes. It streaked down her cheek. "You want a bride," she said, pushing aside the tray to climb out of bed. "And I don't want to be your bride."

Not unless he loved her as much as she loved him. She couldn't believe that was possible—for so many reasons.

Chapter Thirteen

He'd proposed three times in his life. Three more times than his best friend had thought wise. He wished only one of those women had accepted—the one who had actually turned down his proposal.

But if he hadn't married the first woman, he wouldn't have his children. And if the second woman hadn't accepted his proposal, he never would have met Brenna—the woman he really loved, the woman who would never believe that he loved her and didn't just want a mother for his sons.

Frustration had his hand shaking as he reached for his cell phone. "Hello." A feminine voice emanated from the cell.

"This is Josh Towers…"

"Dr. Towers, I'm so glad you called," gushed Mrs. Applewhite. "I was hoping that you would…"

"I'd like to meet with you," he admitted. "But to discuss relisting the house." Nothing else. He'd learned his lesson with women—he would never understand them. He could have sworn Brenna loved him, but apparently not enough to trust him—not enough to trust that he loved her, too.

The Realtor drew in an audible breath, obviously shocked. "You're going to relist?"

"Yes." He had finally accepted that what Nick had told him the day of the wedding-that-wasn't was true. There was nothing in Cloverville for him. How ironic that Nick had found something there—a life, a love. But Josh had lost everything he'd wanted. Colleen wanted Nick to keep his condo in Grand Rapids, that was close to the hospital. Josh's change in plans wouldn't affect her and Nick. Only him and the boys. "And as soon as the office is done, I'd like to have you list that, too."

A gasp was uttered behind him. He glanced over his shoulder to the female Kelly standing in the doorway between the mudroom and the kitchen. Not Brenna. He doubted she intended to come around him again. Her mother, with her wavy white hair and soft brown eyes, stood behind him. She must have dropped off the boys from the zoo. Instead of being tired from the trip, they were running around the backyard, squealing and giggling as they chased Pop. For an old man, he moved surprisingly fast.

"You're not moving," Mama said as if he was her son and he would be forced to obey her.

He spoke into his phone, "Mrs. Applewhite, I'll call you back later."

"Any time," she offered.

"And set up an appointment to discuss business." Business only.

"You don't need an appointment."

He clicked off his cell and dropped it onto the counter. "Mrs. Kelly." He couldn't call her Mama, not since he now wished she would be his mother-in-law. But he had no hope that she would ever be.

"Don't Mrs. Kelly me," she reprimanded him as if she

was talking to one of his boys. "What's this nonsense about your listing the office and the house?"

"I—I have to…"

"You have to stay in Cloverville," she insisted. "Your sons are so happy. They love it here."

His sons loved Brenna Kelly just as he did. Since she didn't want to be part of the lives, wasn't it better to make a clean break? Like their mother had?

Josh sighed. "I want more for them. I wanted to give them a real home. A real family."

"This is your home, Josh," Mama insisted. "This house. This town. This family. Pop and me and Brenna. We're your family now."

He had parents. Like Brenna's, they were madly in love with each other, causing him to grow up under the illusion that he could one day find that kind of love for himself.

"I've grown really fond of all of you," Josh admitted.

"Just fond?" Mama asked, arching a brow.

"Okay, more than fond," he admitted, with a heavy sigh, "but it doesn't matter. She can't get past the fact that I proposed to Molly first."

"Brenna has some self-esteem issues," her mother shared.

"Brenna?" Josh snorted. "I've never met a more self-confident woman."

"She's a self-confident woman on the outside," Mama agreed, "but somewhere deep inside she's also the little girl who was called fat her entire childhood. She has accepted who she is, and she's proud of herself. But because she endured so many insults and so much rejection, she doesn't trust anyone but her family and friends to accept her."

"I'd hoped we were friends."

"You're more than friends," Mama said. "That's why

she will struggle the hardest to believe that *you*, of all people, accept her as she is."

"That I love her," Josh said. "She doesn't believe that I love her."

"And packing up and going back to Grand Rapids is going to convince her?" Mama scoffed.

Josh groaned. He'd figured Brenna would be happy if he left—and left her alone—since she didn't believe in his love. Of course he hadn't been thinking clearly. He'd been hurting too much from her rejecting his proposal.

"No, running away isn't going to convince her," he admitted with the same sense of guilt and shame he'd admitted to Mrs. Hoolihan that he, not Nick, had been the one to shoot the spit balls into Sally Kruger's hair. Of course the woman, like Brenna, hadn't believed him; she'd thought he'd only confessed to cover for his friend.

"No, running away is only going to make her think she was right," Mama said, then sighed. "I don't know what will convince her that you truly love her."

"Your daughter is a stubborn woman," Josh said, unable to keep from grinning. "But if you and Pop are willing to help me again, I think I might have another idea."

Mama smiled and slapped her hands against his cheeks, squeezing like Nick's grandma used to when Josh had been no bigger than his sons were now. "There's my boy! You stay and fight or you're not man enough for my daughter."

"Oh, I'm man enough. I'm the only man for Brenna." He just had to prove it to her.

UNLIKE MOST OF THE BUSINESSES in Cloverville, the bakery opened on Sunday but just for the morning. Brenna unlocked her office after one, when the bakery was closed and empty. She inhaled a deep breath of air, sweet with the lingering scents of cinnamon and chocolate and baking bread. She loved this place so much, but it wasn't enough. She'd decided already that she needed more in her life—she needed Josh and Buzz and TJ.

Had she been a fool to reject his proposal? Should she have settled for the same loveless marriage he'd proposed to Molly? Except it wouldn't have been loveless on her part. And she doubted she was strong enough to handle the disappointment of loving a man who didn't love her back…

As she pushed open the door to her office, a noise drew her attention to the kitchen in the back. A clunk and a thud echoed down the hallway.

"Hello?" she called out.

Another clang reverberated. She recognized the clatter of pots and pans. Even though Cloverville was relatively crime-free, the bakery had an alarm system. An intruder wouldn't be able to get inside. But she trembled slightly with fear as she walked into the industrial kitchen, nearly every bit of it shining stainless steel but for the sparkling white-tiled floor. A man bent over one of the counters, bits of red frosting spattered in his dark hair and a smear across his cheek.

Brenna's heart slammed against her ribs. "Josh?"

He turned toward her. "Oh, you're early. Just give me a minute."

"I'm early?" She lifted an eyebrow. "This is my business. What are you doing here? I thought you'd gone back home."

"I am home." He tossed out the comment, his attention on whatever was on the table, not on her.

"What?"

"Well, not the bakery. This isn't home." He cursed his breath and smeared another trace of red frosting along his jaw. "But Cloverville. Cloverville is home."

"But Mama and Pop said you were selling the house." Her heart pounded harder—with hope. "And the office. That you had decided to move back to Grand Rapids. Or was that another lie?" She hadn't thought so, not when Mama had backed up Pop's claim.

"It *was* the truth." He uttered a sigh of obvious self-disgust. "I had a weak moment."

Brenna could identify. She'd had many weak moments around him. "So you were really going to list it? The house that we worked so hard on?"

He nodded. "That was why. *You* are everywhere—on every wall, in every hinge. How could I live in that house without you?"

"Josh…" God, she hoped he wouldn't propose again. Because she was having weak moment and she just might accept. She just might agree to his marriage of convenience.

"You're probably mad that if I wasn't going to keep it that I hadn't offered it to you first," he said. "But I was mad at you."

"Josh, you have to understand why I couldn't accept your proposal. You barely know me," she reasoned with him. "How can you be sure that you want to spend the rest of your life with me?"

His mouth lifted in a wicked grin as he insisted, "I *know* you."

Her face heated. "Sure, we had sex. We shouldn't have had sex…"

"We didn't have sex," he interrupted. "We made love. I love you and you love me. That's why I proposed."

She shook her head. "You don't love me."

"Why?" he asked. "Why *can't* I love you?"

"Wh-what?" she stammered.

If Josh had had any doubts that an insecure little girl still lived inside this beautiful, confident woman, he had no doubts any more. "Why do you think I don't love you?"

Her shoulders, bare since she wore a sleeveless green dress, lifted in a shrug. "We only met a little over two weeks ago."

"In person," he reminded her. "But we've been talking on the phone and e-mailing for weeks."

"Planning your wedding to my best friend," she said, her husky voice thick with irony.

"It should have been *our* wedding we were planning."

"It w-was Molly's wedding."

"Oh, she made the decisions? She chose the color of the dresses, the flowers?" he persisted, then laughed when she shook her head, conceding that her friend had had no involvement.

She lifted her chin and insisted, "*You* chose the dresses, the flowers."

He laughed again. "Like I chose the paint colors for my house."

Her alabaster skin flushed bright pink, but then she shrugged again. "I can't help that I have good taste."

"Yes, you do." Josh grinned. "You love me."

"Stop saying that."

"You're not denying it," he pointed out. "You're just denying that *I* can love *you*. And I want to know why you think I can't."

"You're just looking for a mother for your sons. That's why you proposed to Molly," she reminded him. "And that's why you proposed to me."

"I love Buzz and TJ," he said, "so of course I would do anything to make them happy—even propose to a woman I didn't love. I figured the friendship Molly and I had begun could develop into love. And that it would be less complicated and eventually stronger than a relationship begun on attraction only."

"I know. You explained that."

"I was right," he said, proud that he hadn't been wrong about everything. "A relationship begun with friendship is stronger, more secure than one based on lust alone."

Brenna rubbed her forehead as if her head was spinning. "I don't understand…"

"You and I began a friendship, through those calls and e-mails." He'd loved the sexiness of her voice, and the humor of her witty e-mails. "I can't tell you how much I looked forward to talking to you and how excited I was to meet you in person."

He blew out a shaky breath at the memory of the first time he'd seen her, the sun glowing like fire in her red hair. "And then when I did, the attraction was instant. With you I found everything I was ever looking for."

"A mother for your sons."

He pressed a finger over her lips. "Don't. You know me better than that. I was honest with Molly about my feelings. Why would I lie to *you*?"

Brenna closed her eyes tight, trying to control the rapid beat of her hopeful heart. Josh wasn't a liar; she knew he'd only ever been honest with Molly and her. "Okay, maybe you do think you love me. But you were wrong before, about Amy."

"I was young and stupid," he said. "I know better now. I know what love is. I know what it feels like. I feel it for my children. I feel it for you."

Despite keeping her eyes closed, a tear streaked from beneath one lid.

"And I feel it *from* you," he continued. "I feel your love for me. If I can't love you, why can you love me?"

"You're perfect." She opened her eyes and stared up into his face, as always awed by just how good-looking he was.

"You're gorgeous," she said. "And smart. And funny. And successful. You can have any woman you want." Except for Molly. She suspected Molly wanted Eric. At least she hoped her friends would finally get together. "Why would you want me?"

"Oh, Brenna…" He reached for her, pulling her into his arms.

She pressed her palms against his chest, keeping herself from melting into him. "I'm not perfect, Josh. You're a cosmetic surgeon. You're used to perfection."

"Yes. So I know it when I see it. You are perfect, Brenna, exactly as you are."

"I'm real." She repeated the compliment he'd given her, the one that had touched her so. "But you'll get bored with that, you'll want me to be something I'm not."

Josh touched his forehead to hers. "Oh, Brenna. I love you—as you are. I wouldn't change one thing about you. Well, except…"

She fisted her hands against his chest. "Except what?" Her hips probably.

"How damned stubborn you are. Or maybe your bossiness." He shook his head. "No, I wouldn't even change those. I love everything about you, Brenna Kelly."

"I'm not going to lose weight," she warned him. "I've tried. Diets make me ornery. I can't run. I won't jog. At the most I walk." She shook her head. "No, I stroll. Mama and I take a stroll every night. Good for the heart, you know."

"I know. I am a doctor," he said.

"A plastic surgeon," she said. "I'm not plastic. I'm never going to be Barbie."

"I don't want to marry Barbie. I want to marry you."

God help her she was beginning to believe him. "Josh…"

"I thought you were so confident, so self-assured," he *tsked* as if disappointed in her.

"I am." Except with him. Something about him made her feel like that insecure fat girl she'd once been.

"You don't see yourself the way I see you," Josh said. "You're beautiful." He turned her in his arms, so she could finally see what he'd been working on at the counter.

"Oh…" She laughed. "You did this?"

"Pop and Mama helped. They gave me the recipe and watched so that I didn't screw it up." He grinned with pride. "But I decorated it entirely on my own."

She reached up and swiped a finger across the frosting on his jaw. "I can see that."

And she could see that he loved her—in the cake he'd decorated for her, molded and frosted in her curvy image. Red hair fell in waves over creamy white shoulders, big breasts and rounded hips. A laugh bubbled out from between her lips. "You made me an X-rated cake."

"It's you."

"I can see that." Was the man talented at everything he did?

"That's how I see you."

"It really is beautiful," she acknowledged. "Are you sure you're not a sculptor instead of a surgeon?"

"I'm a man in love. I love you, Brenna Kelly. I'll love you forever," he promised. "Now let's have some cake."

She shook her head. "I don't want to mess it up. It's too…perfect."

"There's always room for cake," he reminded her. "So go ahead. Mess it up. And any time you forget how beautiful you are, I can make you another."

"No. All I have to do is look into your eyes." And she could see herself as he saw her.

He expelled a ragged breath. "You believe me. You finally believe that I love you."

She nodded. "I'm stubborn. Not stupid."

"Stop being stubborn and have some cake."

She stepped closer to the table, admiring every curvy line of the cake. "It's…" She noted something glittering in the belly button of the cake version of Brenna. "What's that? I don't have a belly button ring." She turned toward him, lifting her eyebrow once again as she asked, "Do you want me to get one?"

"Take it out," he advised her.

Brenna reached for the glittering stone and pulled out a diamond ring. "Josh!"

"I decided to go ahead and pick it out myself," he said. "I figured, since I'd bought the house you wanted, and you and I like the same colors, that we probably have similar taste."

She would have absolutely picked the oval diamond with the platinum band for herself. Tears stung her eyes at its sparkling beauty.

"Will you let me put *this* ring on your finger?" he asked.

She nodded and held out her hand. After licking off the band, he slid the ring onto her finger. And she sighed. "It fits."

"Perfectly. Just like us."

"I love you," she said as emotion overflowed her full heart.

Josh tapped the diamond on her hand. "So you'll marry me."

"Yes."

He looked at her with suspicion. "Are you marrying me just to get your hands on my house?"

"Nope."

He tilted his jaw, studying her. "Because you want to mother my sons?"

She smiled. "Nope. I'm marrying you because I want my hands on you. Every night for the rest of our lives. I love you so much, Joshua Towers."

"Not nearly as much as I love you," he said, kissing her lips, then her shoulder. Then kissing wasn't enough, and they made love right there in the bakery kitchen.

As she straightened her clothes, Josh swiped a smear of frosting from her cheek. "Mmmm…you're right. There is always room for cake."

She slapped at his chest. "You're bad." No, he was good. *Very good*. And she was one lucky woman.

He pulled her close, hugging her to his chest. "So how long will it take you to plan another wedding?"

Brenna smiled.

"What?"

"We may have to wait our turn. Abby and Clayton are getting married," she shared.

Josh grinned. "And Nick and Colleen."

"Really?"

"He asked me to be his best man," Josh said, beaming with pride.

"Then there's Molly."

Brenna sighed. She was worried about her best friend. Neither she nor Eric had seemed too hopeful about their future—alone or together.

"She'll find the man she's meant to marry," Josh assured her.

Brenna nodded. "She already did."

In the second grade, Eric had proposed to her. Maybe Molly would finally hold him to that promise just as Brenna intended to hold Josh to his, to love her forever.

Epilogue

Josh closed his hand over Brenna's, and together they sliced through the first layer of cake. Their wedding cake: five frosted tiers, on the top of which stood a proud plastic groom in his tuxedo with his molded dark hair and his bright smile. Next to him, their plastic hands joined, stood his redheaded bride. Josh grinned, pleased the groom no longer stood alone. Then he redirected his attention, and his heart swelled with pride and love as he gazed down at his beautiful bride.

Brenna handed him a slice, then lifted the piece she held to his lips. He lifted his slice, teasing her lips with the frosted sweetness. Together, they bit into the cake.

While the wedding party and rest of the guests, pretty much the entire town of Cloverville, cheered and called out for them to smash it into each other's face, they only smiled at each other. Then Josh leaned forward and kissed the frosting off Brenna's mouth. Breathless, he pulled away and nuzzled her neck, whispering into her ear, "I'd like the cake better if it was of you."

He'd only had to sculpt that one in her image. She hadn't needed any reminders of how beautiful she was or of how much he loved her.

"Don't let Pop hear you," his bride warned him.

He nodded, seeing as how Pop had his knife, deftly slicing up the rest of the cake, which Mama, using a little silver spatula, was placing on small plates.

"Where are the candles?" Buzz asked.

TJ bumped his shoulder against his twin's, jostling him dangerously close to the table. "It's not a birthday cake, stupid."

Josh's bride crouched near her new stepsons. "You can make a wish if you want to," she told Buzz.

"Me, too?" TJ asked.

"You can both make a wish." She'd always known, instinctively, how to handle his competitive boys.

"Did *you* make a wish?" Buzz asked her.

She smiled down at the twins, her green eyes shining with love. "I already have everything I want."

Buzz closed his eyes, puckered his lips and blew out a breath as if he were blowing out candles. TJ elbowed him but then copied his brother's actions.

"What did you wish for?" Josh asked his sons, hoping that, like him and Brenna, his boys had everything they wanted. He knew they had everything they needed.

The boys exchanged one of *their* glances, then TJ answered for them both. "We wished for a little sister."

"What?" Josh asked, stunned. "A sister?"

"Yeah," Buzz agreed, gesturing toward the flower girl, Lara Hamilton-McClintock. "Girls aren't so bad. When we were getting our pictures taken in the park, Lara sat on TJ and made him eat a worm."

Yet the little blond girl hadn't even a smudge on the white dress she'd worn for so many weddings while his boys' rented tuxedoes were grass-stained and fraying at the knees and hems.

Instead of parental outrage, amusement bubbled up inside Josh, and he laughed, then winked at Lara. "She looks so sweet," he murmured to Brenna.

"But she's tough."

"Like you. Sweet and strong." He grinned. "I think I'm with the boys. I'd love to have a daughter—one who looks just like her mama with red hair and green eyes."

Brenna laughed as the boys ran off with the slices of cake they'd snagged from the table the minute Pop had cut them. "You all have no idea what you're getting into. She could be bossy and stubborn," she warned him of their "daughter."

"I hope so," Josh said, "then she'll really be like her mama."

She rubbed a hand over the satin and lace covering the slight swell of her stomach. She would have never believed she could be as happy as she was on this day—her wedding day. "I guess we'll find out in about five and a half months."

Josh's jaw dropped. "We're having a baby?"

She nodded. "I think I got pregnant that day at the bakery."

"You didn't tell me," he accused her.

"I was saving it for your wedding present."

His blue eyes sparkling with happiness, he brushed a stray curl back from her face. "I didn't need a present. All I need is you."

"Me, too, but we have so much more," she mused as she watched her sons run in circles around the cake table, the guests and the members of the wedding party, who were clad again in black tuxedoes and red dresses.

Josh took her hand and led her to the middle of the dance floor of the American Legion Hall, which had been decorated with red and white fairy lights. It looked as beautiful as that first night she had danced with this man, who was now *her* groom.

They danced the first dance alone, Brenna melting into the strong arms of her husband. For the next song, the rest of the wedding party filed out to join them. The best man danced with a brown-haired bridesmaid. Colleen stared up at her husband, her eyes brimming with love, while Nick, handsome face soft with adoration, stared down at his wife.

Clayton McClintock danced with the two females in his life. Lara, whom he had officially adopted, balanced on one arm while his other encircled his beautiful wife. Abby looked up at him, her eyes alight with a mischievous glint, as she absently stroked her free hand over the swell of her belly beneath her red gown. She and Brenna were due about the same time, but because she was so petite she showed more. She'd even been showing in her wedding dress over a month ago, but she hadn't cared what the town or anyone else thought. She had never been happier.

Like Brenna herself. She slid her fingers into the soft, dark hair brushing Josh's nape. "I love you…"

"And I love you, wife." He kissed her lips as the music ended. Before they could walk off the dance floor, Brenna's matron of honor caught them.

"Time to throw the garter and the bouquet," Molly said, her brown eyes shining as she obviously enjoyed bossing around Brenna for a change. "But I don't know who's left to catch it…"

Even Mrs. McClintock was finally remarried, to their old English teacher.

"I know," Brenna said as she searched the crowd of wedding guests for a distinctive, wide-brimmed hat bedecked with flowers. Mrs. Hild, the long-widowed town busybody, held onto Nick's dad's arm. The charming old guy, who'd also been widowed a long time ago, guided her off the dance floor.

Molly clapped her hands together. "Of course. The Mc-Clintocks' matchmaking ways have rubbed off on you."

Brenna squeezed her best friend's hand. "They've done more than that. They've given me more happiness than I ever thought possible."

Josh, standing yet at her side, hugged them both—the bride who'd jilted him, and the one who would never leave him. And who would love him just as deeply and eternally as he loved her.

* * * * *

So what did happen to Molly?
Find out why she ran out on her wedding—
and meet the man she truly loves.
The exciting conclusion of
THE WEDDING PARTY *miniseries,*
FINALLY A BRIDE,
will be available in October 2008,
only from Harlequin American Romance!

The Colton family is back!
Enjoy a sneak preview of
COLTON'S SECRET SERVICE by Marie Ferrarella,
part of THE COLTONS: FAMILY FIRST *miniseries.*

Available from Silhouette Romantic Suspense
in September 2008.

He cautioned himself to be leery. He was human and he'd been conned before. But never by anyone nearly so attractive. Never by anyone he'd felt so attracted to.

In her defense, Nick supposed that Georgie could actually be telling him the truth. That she was a victim in all this. He had his people back in California checking her out, to make sure she was who she said she was and had, as she claimed, not even been near a computer but on the road these last few months that the threats had been made.

In the meantime, he was doing his own checking out. Up close and exceedingly personal. So personal he could feel his blood stirring.

It had been a long time since he'd thought of himself as anything other than a law enforcement agent of one type or other. But Georgeann Grady made him remember that beneath the oaths he had taken and his devotion to duty, there beat the heart of a man.

A man who'd been far too long without the touch of a woman.

He watched as the light from the fireplace caressed the outline of Georgie's small, trim, jean-clad body as she moved about the rustic living room that could have easily come off the set of a Hollywood Western. Except that it was genuine.

As genuine as she claimed to be?

Something inside of him hoped so.

He wasn't supposed to be taking sides. His only interest in being here was to guarantee Senator Joe Colton's safety as the latter continued to make his bid for the presidency. Everything else was supposed to be secondary, but, Nick had to silently admit, that was just a wee bit hard to remember right now.

Earlier, before she'd put her precocious handful of a daughter to bed, Georgie had fed his appetite by whipping up some kind of a delicious concoction out of the vegetables she'd pulled from her garden. Vegetables that, by all rights, should have been withered and dried. She'd mentioned that a friend came by on occasion to weed and tend it. Still, it surprised him that somehow she'd managed to make something mouthwatering out of it.

Almost as mouthwatering as she looked to him right at this moment.

Again, he was reminded of the appetite that hadn't been fed, hadn't been satisfied.

And wasn't going to be, Nick sternly told himself. At least not now. Maybe later, when things took on a more definite shape and all the questions in his head were answered to his satisfaction, there would be time to explore this feeling. This woman. But not now.

Damn it.

"Sorry about the lack of light," Georgie said, breaking into his train of thought as she turned around to face him. If she noticed the way he was looking at her, she gave no indication. "But I don't see a point in paying for electricity if I'm not going to be here. Besides, Emmie really enjoys camping out. She likes roughing it."

"And you?" Nick asked, moving closer to her, so close that a whisper would have trouble fitting in. "What do you like?"

The very breath stopped in Georgie's throat as she looked up at him.

"I think you've got a fair shot of guessing that one," she told him softly.

* * * * *

*Be sure to look for COLTON'S SECRET SERVICE
and the other following titles from*
THE COLTONS: FAMILY FIRST *miniseries:*
RANCHER'S REDEMPTION by Beth Cornelison
THE SHERIFF'S AMNESIAC BRIDE by Linda Conrad
SOLDIER'S SECRET CHILD by Caridad Piñeiro
BABY'S WATCH by Justine Davis
A HERO OF HER OWN by Carla Cassidy

Romantic
SUSPENSE

**Sparked by Danger,
Fueled by Passion.**

The Coltons Are Back!

Marie Ferrarella
Colton's Secret Service

The Coltons: Family First

On a mission to protect a senator, Secret Service agent
Nick Sheffield tracks down a threatening message only
to discover Georgie Gradie Colton, a rodeo-riding single
mom, who insists on her innocence. Nick is instantly
taken with the feisty redhead, but vows not to let his
feelings interfere with his mission. Now he must figure
out if this woman is conning him or if he can trust her
and the passion they share....

Available September wherever books are sold.

**Look for upcoming Colton titles
from Silhouette Romantic Suspense:**

RANCHER'S REDEMPTION by Beth Cornelison, Available October
THE SHERIFF'S AMNESIAC BRIDE by Linda Conrad, Available November
SOLDIER'S SECRET CHILD by Caridad Piñeiro, Available December
BABY'S WATCH by Justine Davis, Available January 2009
A HERO OF HER OWN by Carla Cassidy, Available February 2009

Visit Silhouette Books at www.eHarlequin.com   SRS27598

REQUEST YOUR FREE BOOKS!

2 FREE NOVELS PLUS 2
FREE GIFTS!

American ★ Romance®

Heart, Home & Happiness!

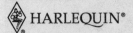

HARLEQUIN®

American ★ Romance®

COMING NEXT MONTH

#1225 A DAD FOR HER TWINS by Tanya Michaels
The State of Parenthood
Kenzie Green is starting over—new job, new city, new house—to provide a better life for her nine-year-old twins. Unfortunately, the house isn't finished yet, so the three of them temporarily move into an apartment across the hall from the mysterious and gorgeous Jonathan Trelauney. Watching her kids open up to JT is enthralling…thinking of him as a father to her twins is irresistible!

#1226 TEXAS HEIR by Linda Warren
Cari Michaels has been in love with the newly engaged Reed Preston, CEO and heir to a family-owned Texas chain of department stores, for a long time. When their plane crashes in desolate west Texas—and help doesn't arrive—they start the long trek to civilization. Once they're rescued, will Reed follow through with his engagement...or marry the woman who has captured his heart?

#1227 SMOKY MOUNTAIN HOME by Lynnette Kent
Ruth Ann Blakely has worked in the stables at The Hawksridge School for most of her life. Her attachment to the students she teaches, to her horses and to the stables themselves is unshakeable. So when architect Jonah Granger is hired to build new a stable for the school—and tear the old one down—he's in for a fight. But Jonah isn't a man who's easy to say no to....

#1228 A FIREFIGHTER IN THE FAMILY by Trish Milburn
When Miranda "Randi" Cooke is assigned to investigate a fire in her hometown, she not only has to face her estranged family but also her ex-boyfriend Zac Parker. As the case heats up, Randi finds she needs Zac's help. While they're working closely together, her feelings for Zac are rekindled—but can the tough arson investigator forgive old hurts and learn to trust again?

www.eHarlequin.com